CLOSED SYSTEM

by Zach Hughes

A SIGNET BOOK

NEW AMERICAN LIBRARY

NAL BOOKS ARE AVAILABLE AT QUANTITY DISCOUNTS
WHEN USED TO PROMOTE PRODUCTS OR SERVICES.
FOR INFORMATION PLEASE WRITE TO PREMIUM MARKETING DIVISION,
NEW AMERICAN LIBRARY, 1633 BROADWAY,
NEW YORK, NEW YORK 10019.

SIGNET TRADEMARK REG. U.S. PAT. OFF. AND FOREIGN COUNTRIES
REGISTERED TRADEMARK—MARCA REGISTRADA
HECHO EN CHICAGO, U.S.A.

SIGNET, SIGNET CLASSIC, MENTOR, ONYX, PLUME, MERIDIAN
and NAL BOOKS are published by NAL PENGUIN INC.,
1633 Broadway, New York, New York 10019

First Printing, March, 1986

3 4 5 6 7 8 9 10 11

PRINTED IN THE UNITED STATES OF AMERICA

ONE

The computer was being cranky again. The older models of the Century Series were subject to ionization of the Verboldt Cloud memory chambers, and decontamination of the chambers in a well-equipped shop on a civilized planet was the only cure. In the Ophiuchus sector planets were few, even if one counted Van Biesbroeck's brown dwarf, a gas giant circling VB-8, twenty-one light-years out from Old Earth and almost thirteen light-years behind. As for the degree of civilization in Ophiuchus, that remained to be seen.

Pat Howe had the ship's optics on scan. He was sure that he recognized the obverse patterns of stars in both Scorpius and Sagittarius, but when dealing with distances measured in parsecs on the far end of a little-used blink route, one did not rely on optical readings as interpreted by the always fallible human mind.

The computer had begun to develop a crusty personality after the *Skimmer*'s last overhaul. It reminded Pat of a creaking, proud, overly meticulous old man more intent on thoroughness than efficiency. The computer had gone to H-alpha light and was laboriously building a composite 360-degree photo map, following a procedure designed for use in the event a ship became hopelessly lost, with not one known point recognizable. However, sooner or later the computer would accomplish the purpose of checking the ship's position. To halt the process would have required giving the computer detailed instructions, and that would have interrupted Pat's dinner.

The nutrition servos were working well, as were, indeed, all of the ship's systems except the computer. *Skimmer* was a smoothly functioning complex of hardware, electronics, and subatomic technology that muttered, purred, clicked around Pat with familiar, reassuring sounds. She was in excellent condition for her age, squat and squarish, solidly built. She was moderately luxurious inside and all space dog outside, a refitted deep-space tug, Mule Class. She had become surplus, and thus affordable, when the deep-space tug companics began racing each other to replace the dependable old Mules with the sleek, ultrapowerful Greyhounds.

For five decades, the Mules had been the most reliable ships in space. *Skimmer* had power to spare in her drive system, because she'd been built to be able to haul in the largest liner, and to be able to make multiple blinks without recharging the oversized blink generator which, with the chambers of the flux atmospace drive, occupied a large portion of her interior space.

As the computer built its maps on the screen, the nearer stars appeared as haloed, sparkling points of light. Pat slid his plate back into the nutrition servo, put his feet up on the console, and mused idly as the Carina Nebula formed on the screen, its emission nebulosity only slightly altered in shape from the familiar pattern on United Planets—oriented maps. He was a man at home with himself and his world, a world which consisted of the *Skimmer*, his library, his own thoughts.

Pat Howe was a sandy blond man, not only in hair coloration but in skin pigmentation. He was a bit thin for his six feet, but hard-muscled, staying fit through religiously observed exercise periods both in null-gravity and in the ship's easily activated artificial gravity. Some took him to be in his late twenties. Others would guess that he was nearing forty. Actually, he was thirty-five and, because of his emotional stability and his relatively new freedom, expected to live past that biblically promised age of sixscore years.

The computer whirred, an electronic chuckle. "You're gonna make it yet," Pat said, as the Jewel Box, the galactic cluster Kappa Crucis, formed on the screen. From the *Skimmer*'s point of reference, the Jewel Box had been glaringly evident to a quick scan.

The computer, almost chortling, leaped with its old swiftness to place *Skimmer* just under two light-years out from the single star wing of the Ophiuchus group, just where they were supposed to be.

"Congratulations," Pat said, as the computer delivered coordinates for orbital approach to Taratwo. Now that he had the coordinates, he was in no hurry to use them. His mind was not quite prepared for action.

There were times when it seemed best to postpone action in favor of some thinking, and Pat was a man who believed in following his hunches.

The computer flashed a green light at him, bragging about a job finished and well done.

"Just hold your horses," Pat said. He punched

up a cup of steaming coffee, with cream and sugar, from the servo and sat easily, feet up, the mug heating both hands as he clasped it. There was no urgent reason for his hesitation, no clang-clang of warning in his skull, just a reluctance to push the button and send the *Skimmer* on to her destination. No harm, he decided, in going over it one more time.

The ship's papers, and his own, were in order. He was Audrey Patricia Howe, an accredited free trader, bonded to carry cargo of all classes up to Class AAA pharmaceuticals, of which his current cargo consisted. To carry the potent drugs in *Skimmer*'s storage areas required a half-dozen permits and licenses, for in the wrong hands the drugs could produce happy times and headaches. Properly handled, his cargo was as legal as a church.

Was that the problem?

He'd had to express his concern in a polite way to the businessmen on Zcdc II who had commissioned him. At first he'd gotten the idea that they had something other than legal Class AAA in mind. There'd been nothing concrete or overt, just hints that very profitable items could be carried by an accredited trader to an independent out-planet.

Needless to say, he was having nothing to do with illegal drugs. UP law might not be present as far out as Taratwo, but Pat had no intention of spending his life in the cosmic outback, no intention of risking a negative entry on his record on any planet, no matter how far removed from UP Central.

So the cargo was legal, and he had the right papers to carry it. He had done what a trader always strives to do. He had bought cheap and he would sell dear, and the profit from the cargo would be a welcome bonus to the fee he'd set on the commission from the businessmen on Zede II.

Thinking of the size of that fee gave him two emotions, joy and happiness. Half of it was already on deposit in his account in the UP Bank and Trust Company on Xanthos. The other half was on demand deposit on Zede II, requiring only a coded affirmative from the men who had chartered *Skimmer* to be transferred to his account. That coded affirmative would be sent before he delivered a certain item of cargo to an isolated, private landing pad on Zede II.

The computer blinked its green light again. "Take a break," Pat said, but he let his feet slide off the console, and leaned forward to punch the stand-by button on the computer.

On the surface, it was to be a simple operation. All he had to do was blink out to a distant planet in the Ophiuchus sector. He would be contacted on landing by a friend of his employers on Zede II. He would trade his cargo, pick up a passenger, whose legality had been sworn to by the Zede II businessmen, and take that passenger back. Such a simple mission could have been performed more economically and more comfortably for the passenger by any charter yacht in the UP system.

And that, he decided, was why he was hesitating.

The Zedeians, two of them, neatly dressed in the standard tailored suits of businessmen, had sought him in his small office on Xanthos, having made a trip of twenty parsecs from the Zede suns. When he realized that they'd deliberately chosen him, a man with a cannon, to do a job which could have been done by an unarmed yacht, he had begun to wonder.

"Why do you need an armed mercenary?" he had asked.

"The passenger is important," the spokesman for the businessmen had said. "We want the passenger to have every possible degree of safety."

"From what?" Pat had asked.

"It is a lonely and desolate part of the galaxy. There have been pirate attacks there."

But there hadn't been a recorded act of piracy since X&A had sent fifty ships of the line to reduce the pirate strongholds on the Hogg Moons.

When Pat didn't like a proposition, he set the fee impossibly high. He had named a figure, knowing that it would be refused, and without blinking an eye the Zedeians had accepted. Obviously, there was more to the proposition than appeared on the surface. But it was a lot of money. Pat liked his freedom, and without financial freedom there is no personal freedom. And, after all, he was paid to take risks.

"Just what business are you in?" Pat had asked.

"We are involved in several areas," the spokesman had said. "Import-export, for example. Recently we've become interested in producing entertainment films."

Just plain, ordinary businessmen. Businessmen who were willing to spend a small fortune without even bargaining over the price to send a legally armed mercenary on a simple passenger-carrying mission. The problem was that there was nothing simple about anything Zedeian. It had been a thousand years since the prosperous, populous Zede worlds had engaged in their last war of conquest, but historians, to whom Pat had been often exposed, talked about "the War" as if it had happened yesterday. For a while, during that last of man's big wars, the first all-out war in space, it had been anyone's victory, touch and go. In desperation, the free worlds of the United Planets Confederation had used a terrible new weapon, the planet reducer, for the first and last time in recorded history. Seven Zede planets were ruptured, blown apart, sent flying into space in chunks and pieces, all life destroyed, before the Zede warlords capitulated.

UP historians justified the use of the planet destroyer by saying that freedom had been preserved, that millions of lives had been spared by ending the war. Some historians and moralists went all the way back to the mid-twentieth century to find historical precedents.

The peace treaty had been generous. The surviving Zede worlds had become a semiautonomous part of the Confederation, a status which continued into modern times. UP laws governed all the Zede planets, but the Zedeians were notoriously independent, and sometimes rather frustratingly inventive. Zede led the Confederation in innovative industrial development, in subatomic technology. The Vervoldt Cloud memory chambers which had given a relatively small shipboard computer the storage capacity and reasoning ability of a somewhat backward human brain had been developed on Zede's Valhalla. The advanced weapons which were mounted on the latest ships of the UP Fleet and the ship of the Department of Exploration and Alien Search, were largely Zedeian. The arms trade, indeed, was at the core of Zede's prosperity, big business within the UP, a profitable sideline when dealing with non-aligned, independent planets of which there were very few, and those mostly on the far fringes of the explored and charted portion of the galaxy.

Had the Zede "businessmen" had a small shipment of arms in mind when they hinted at a more profitable cargo for the *Skimmer*? Pat didn't think so. Armaments were often bulky. The store of Class AAA drugs in *Skimmer*'s storage areas was, Pat felt, just about the most profitable cargo he could carry, for you could pack a lot of high-class medicine into a small space.

Pat had taken the *Skimmer* to Zede II to buy his cargo, having been assured of the lowest prices in the Confederation. He'd done some talking around the port, and the word was that a man with the right connnections could buy just about anything he wanted to buy somewhere on Zede II. It was there that he had heard repeated a persistent rumor, unproven as yet, that someone was dealing in the filth of the old nuclear weapons, and perhaps even the long-since-outlawed planet reducers.

The rumor had leaked originally from the crew of an X&A ship back from charting a new blink route in search of always scarce habitable planets. A long way from home, in a previously uncharted area, the ship had picked up suspicious readings from a barren, small, Mercury-like planet. The planet, if the X&A ship's analyzers were working properly, had recently, in the past two decades at the most, been the site of hydrogen fusion tests. Since the need for power from either fusion or fission had been eliminated soon after the first starship went out from Old Earth, there was only one possible use for the nasty power of the atom. nuclear power was good only for destruction, and not even efficient destruction. An X&A destroyer had more firepower than a thousand hydrogen bombs. If someone had been playing around with the antique nuclear weapons their intent could only be blackmail. Livable planets were rare, widely scattered. The constantly multiplying populations of the UP worlds made X&A's search for new living space the most important function of government. A madman with nuclear bombs, threatening to make a life-zone planet unlivable with slowly decaying radioactivity would be in a powerful position.

All of these old thoughts replayed through Pat's mind as he sat, scratching himself. That was a small but important luxury, to be able to scratch where he itched when he itched and not worry about couth. He liked living alone.

He grinned at the computer. "Give me the display file on Taratwo," he said.

The computer disliked oral orders. It fancied itself an old man, hearing becoming impaired. He had to repeat the order, loudly. The computer muttered to itself for a few seconds, punished him by taking extra seconds to check and crosscheck all references to the planet Taratwo, then delivered the file to the screen.

Pat had examined the file a dozen times on the trip out. He had in his data banks all the information available on Taratwo, fourth planet of the star Upsilon Ophiuchus. He had data not available in the public banks, thanks to Jeanny Thompson.

A few years back, when Pat was enduring tenure in the Roget Seat of Philology at Xanthos University, both he and Jeanny had thought that an alliance between learning and practical science, between the learned professor and the upwardly mobile X&A technician, might work. Neither of them could remember the moment of mutal decision, nor place blame, for the realization that a permanent marriage would be undesirable.

Jeanny just bent the rules a little bit when she allowed Pat access to X&A's file on Taratwo.

"That's a long way from home," Jeanny had said, when he made his needs known.

"That makes it interesting," Pat had said.

They had read the file together as it slid silently from the printer.

"If I were you, boy, I'd walk easy out there," Jeanny said. "That planet is an anachronism. An absolute ruler in this enlightened, unquote, age?"

Taratwo had been discovered by accident and peopled by political dissidents who had carefully nursed on their journey through space an old, old grudge from the Old Earth, a grudge so ancient that the reason for it was a long-forgotten mystery. When a race can lose its home planet for thousands of years the reasons behind a simple little family fight among tribes of men can also be lost.

"This is interesting," Jeanny had said. "The name of the planet is taken from the site of the palace of a legendary race of kings, back on Old Earth."

Pat had been more interested in solid information. Taratwo's political status was Independent. There were no organized trade routes to any UP planet, but there were records of trips to the planet by free traders. The autocratic ruler of Taratwo didn't call himself a king, but according to all information he was the boss, the absolute ruler.

"He fancies himself to be a great leader," Jeanny had said. "He's a bad dude, Audrey—"

"Don't call me Audrey," Pat had said.

"—standing tall and alone on the frontier of the

inhabited galaxy. And look at this. He's been buying warships from the Zede munitions plants."

The figures were impressive. Taratwo, a small, insignificant planet, had the most powerful fleet arm of any independent planet or group of independent planets.

Pat whistled through his teeth in surprise. It would take a full UP battle fleet to reduce Taratwo's power, and not without loss, because Taratwo had been buying the latest, most powerful ships and weapons, every modern weapon except, of course, reducers.

"Let's run down all recorded trips by free traders," Pat had said, not too concerned about Taratwo's powerful fleet. The *Skimmer* was armed, true, but no one in his right mind would use an entire fleet to chase—if the need arose—one small deep-space tug converted into an armed mercenary.

Taratwo seemed to welcome free traders. Isolated as they were, no established trade routes within a dozen parsecs, free traders would keep them up to date and bring in the latest in, for example, medicines.

There in Jeanny's office at X&A Headquarters on Xanthos, they had stared, together, at a holographic chart of the Taratwo sector. Jeanny shuddered. "It's lonely out there," she'd said.

Pat had nodded, musing. Taratwo was alone, the only populated planet in a twelve-parsec radius of space. She was a relatively new planet, as planetary age goes, and she was, in theory, too small to hold a viable atmosphere. Mountain formation was still going on, and that made for considerable volcanic activity along with the resultant earthquakes. Population was under half a billion. Chief exports were heavy metals and gemstones.

"Well, Audrey," Jeanny had said, "you have picked an odd profession. You can expect odd places and odd people."

"Don't call me Audrey," Pat had said.

"You're a mercenary, a gun for hire," Jeanny had said. "Nice citizens and nice planets don't often need a man with a gun."

"I think of myself as a knight in shining armor." he'd said, "soaring into the nebulous distances of the universe on missions of true and pure good."

"Batshit," Jeanny had said. "It's just a way of running from responsibility."

He had made the statement with a mock look of arrogance on his face, eyes idealistically wide, eyebrows raised, for he would never admit to anyone that he'd been naive enough, in the beginning, to see it just that way when lucky coincidence of birth had made it possible for him to purchase his freedom from the halls of learning and from eager freshmen with an unexpected legacy from an uncle who had been forgotten since he boarded a colony ship aimed for a star near the Coal Sack.

"Knight, hell," Jeanny had said. "You're a bum in an antique space tug which carries enough armament to take on a destroyer."

"For defense against pirates," he'd said, remembering as he said it that the Zede "businessmen" had said much the same thing.

"We blasted the last pirates off the Hogg Moons," Jeanny had said. "Why don't you grow up, Audrey Patricia?"

"Don't call me Audrey Patricia," he'd said, before thanking her for her help.

From Jeanny's office he'd gone directly to UP Central Control. Although space travel was safe, and ships dependable, anything mechanical or electronic or subatomic would break down sooner or later, usually at the most inopportune time. UP Central Control's vast array of computers kept track of every registered ship in UP space, and every registered ship *always* left a flight plan on file with Control, or one of its many outposts scattered throughout populated space. It took two days to get a list of twenty-two ships which had filed flight plans including a stop at Taratwo in the past five years. That was not a lot of traffic, but all the ships had returned safely to home ports.

So, he'd gone over all of it in his mind. He'd reread the file on Taratwo. It was time to do something. He punched orders into the computer.

"OK, old man, let's put it in B for boogie," he said, pushing a button. He felt that eerie moment of disorientation which goes with the territory when power is discharged in the core of a blink generator and a ship ceases to exist at one point in space to exist with an almost immeasurable time lapse at another point.

Upsilon Ophiuchus was a small, yellowish sun glowing weakly at less than one old astronomical unit away from a small, almost barren ball shrouded in volcanic smoke and ash. The sun was too small, too weak, to ever make that sad, barren planet rich and pleasant like the more desirable UP worlds. In fact, when the planet's inner fires cooled a bit over the millennia she'd go cold. Most of her atmosphere would have been bled off into space by that time, and what remained would be frozen in small caps of polar ice. He, of course, would not be around to see that happen, nor would any of the people alive on Taratwo.

He checked the approach instructions for Taratwo and activated the voice communicator. This was a measure of the backwardness of the planet, to have to use audio. At up-to-date facilities, approach was handled efficiently and silently by intercomputer communication.

"Taratwo Space Control, Taratwo Space Control," he sang out, feeling good to be needed, "this is the free trader *Skimmer*. Come in."

"Signal Two, *Skimmer*," said a voice with an odd and rather interesting accent. For a moment his old interest in words and their development and usage was back with him, but he could not identify the accent. He gave the computer instructions to send on the proper wavelength and punched up a cup of coffee with cream and sugar as he heard the only slightly mechanical-sounding voice of the computer send the ship's ID, hull number, registration, licenses, all the numbers and letters assigned by a host of red-tape artists on a thousand planets.

"Signal Two received," said Taratwo Space Control. "Hold one."

Pat waited. He had the coffee cooled just right when the accented voice came again. "*Skimmer*, you are number one for Space Port Old Dublin. Landing instructions follow on channel eleven."

He switched channels, grinning. He was not surprised to be number one for the pad. *Skimmer*'s sensors showed nothing else in near space other than Taratwo's sad excuse for a moon.

Flux thrusters grumbled to break *Skimmer*'s fall into atmosphere. There was a high layer of ash, then a band of relatively clear air, high, before the ship plunged into the lower smoke and ash. Below, the lights of Old Dublin, Taratwo's principal city, were lit, but they could not dispel the appearance of gloom over the planet, the result of the sun's filtered half-light.

"You see, old man, you're in better condition than you thought," Pat said, as *Skimmer* settled onto her assigned pad without so much as a clank.

The ship was alone, squarely squat, sturdy. The pad was at the northern end of the Old Dublin Space Port. Pat had activated the armaments console, sat with the fire director's helmet pushed back loosely on his head. All he had to do was jam the helmet in place and think and the ports would fly open to reveal *Skimmer*'s teeth, instantly ready to defend the ship against unpleasant surprises.

A vehicle separated from a line of one-story buildings at a distance of approximately a mile and came toward the ship. Pat kept power in the generator and in the flux drive, for he was, by nature, a cautious man. The oncoming vehicle did not seem to be armed. There was only one occupant, male, in uniform. Pat activated the sound pickups on the hull as the vehicle drew near and stopped at a respectful distance.

"Captain Audrey Patricia Howe?" The voice was accented like the voice of the Taratwo controller.

"Don't call me—" Pat began automatically, then sighed. "Yes," he said.

"I am Captain John Hook, of Taratwo Customs, at your service, sir. Will you please open your hatches for inspection."

Pat kept the ship on alert as he flipped switches. The main entry hatch hissed open, began to exchange clean ship's air for the murky air of the planet. He met the customs official in the lock, handed over the ship's papers.

"I think we need not stand too much on the formalities, Captain Howe," the white-haired, distinguished-looking man said with a smile. "I see you carry Class AAA drugs. That's good. There's always a ready market for such cargo. If I may presume, I would suggest that you trade for emeralds. There's been a new strike, and the price is down, the gems of first quality."

It was quite unlike a local customs official to give a clue to a favorable trade. "Thank you," Pat said. "I have the cargo manifest on the bridge. I can offer you a cup of coffee while you're looking it over."

"Good, if it's a UP brand," Hook said. "I am especially fond of a certain brand from the planet Zede II. It is called Zede's Pride."

Pat took a quick, closer look at the customs man. He had not expected contact so quickly, and definitely not with a Taratwo official.

"Yes," he said. "I have that brand. It's said that the flavor comes from the peculiar quality of the light of a Zede II sunset, which glows like molten copper."

Hook completed the preset identification formula. "Especially at the winter solstice," he said. "Welcome to Taratwo, Captain Howe."

"Are you the passenger?" Pat asked, thinking that if he was, he might lift off immediately. He could, after all, trade the drugs, if not as favorably as on an out-planet, on the way home. There was something about the aura of semigloom, which deepened as the day died, that made him uneasy.

"No, I am not," Hook said. "Control has sent out word that a free trader has arrived. You can complete your business tomorrow. The passenger will board sometime before sunrise on the day after tomorrow."

Pat felt a little shiver of doubt. If the passenger

was legal, why would he board in the dead of night?

"I'd like the passenger to be aboard tomorrow morning, just in case I finish my trading early."

"Your passenger will board no later than one hour before sunrise on the day after tomorrow," Hook said, and there was a finality in his voice. He smiled again, showing that Taratwo's dentists were a bit behind the times. "You will be number one at the customs shed at one hour after sunrise tomorrow. I will be there. Inspection of your trade goods will be our only point of discussion."

"Got you," Pat said, not liking it, not liking it at all.

Darkness came to Taratwo with a rush. The smoky sky lowered. Just after the stygian dark closed around the ship a tremor rippled the flexible metal grid of the landing pad, causing *Skimmer*'s gyros to whine in adjustment.

Pat set all detectors. The ship was an armed camp. Instruments would detect the approach of whatever passed for a mouse on Taratwo, or the focusing of any sort of beam on the ship.

For his dinner, he selected Tigian dragon's-tail steak and Xanthos salad. He wasn't sleepy. *Skimmer* operated on Xanthos standard time, which did not match Taratwo's time, and he didn't feel like taking a sleeping pill.

As he ate, he checked the ship's film catalog. He'd added several new titles in preparation for the trip, and he'd seen all of them at least once, with the exception of a film which had been given to him on Zede II by his "businessmen" charterers, with a hearty recommendation to enjoy. He hadn't run it because, as a rule, he found Zedeian films to be heavy, often deep in psychological complications which would not have puzzled a Xanthos U. freshman, always gloomy in outlook.

When he punched up the film he was pleasantly surprised. The theme was very Zedeian, but it had interest, if only to show that the Zedeians had a slightly antique view of the role of women in society.

There was nothing wrong with the technical aspects of Zede filmmaking. Zedeians were, after all, the Confederation's finest technicians. The holographic image was almost realistic enough to step into. The acting was surprisingly good. The star of the film was a delicately built redhead with a knockout face and an extraordinary body. The story told of a young woman in love with one man. She was being forced by custom and her parents to marry another. It was a period piece, set in that distant past before the Zedeian war, and as the story progressed Pat began to see and hear references to Zede pride and Zede military strength. The male actors strutted, spoke with an arrogance which was familiar, because, although they were supposed to be historical characters, their thought patterns were the same as those of the Zedeians Pat had known.

He hadn't paid much attention to the credits in the beginning. When the film ended he started it again and looked for the name of the redheaded actress. She was listed as Corinne Tower. When she first appeared she was sweeping down a wide, curving flight of stairs, dressed in formal gown, hair piled atop her head. Pat froze motion, left the miniature woman frozen in space, so lifelike, so much woman. Finally, with a sigh, he turned off the projector.

He went to sleep with ease and dreamed of the redheaded woman. It was a very exciting dream.

TWO

A light, sooty rain delayed dawn. Pat lifted the *Skimmer* on her flux thrusters to land her directly in front of the customs building. Other landing pads were already occupied by pitted and rusted work vessels, long in service, and two new atmospace vehicles. The names of the ships were, of course, in English. It was a one-language galaxy, unless one happened to stumble into an obscure field of esoteric knowledge, the study of extinct languages which had survived in fragments, or of that one alien language which man had encountered in a book which was all that remained of a fascinating civilization out among the colliding galaxies in Cygnus.

While he waited for Captain John Hook and his men to board *Skimmer* to check her cargo, Pat savored the names of the local ships: *Canny Belle*, *Mary's Darlin'*, *Jay-Ann*. The two newer ships apparently belonged to the same company, since the names showed little imagination: *Capcor I* and *Capcor II*.

From appearances, some form of free enterprise existed on Taratwo. Pat guessed correctly that the rusted, battered older ships belonged to independent prospectors or miners.

"You are cleared, Captain," John Hook said, handing over papers to be signed in triplicate. "I have heard that Capcor has eyes for your cargo. They'll go high."

"That's what I like," Pat said. "Thank you again."

He rode the cart which moved his cargo inside the customs shed. There were thieves in customs in more prosperous and civilized places than Old Dublin.

His was the only merchandise inside the huge shed. The customs men helped him offload the cases from the cart. About two dozen men surrounded the platform on which his goods had been placed. He had had the computer print out copies of his cargo manifest. He handed them out, smiling, saying, "Morning, gentlemen."

A tall, well-dressed man with a well-styled head of heavy black hair pushed forward. "Captain, there's no need for that. I am prepared to make you the highest offer. I will take your entire cargo."

Well, why not? He was after the highest price. He owned no obligation to the less well-dressed traders who surrounded the platform. But when he looked into the tall man's eyes he saw coldness. The thin lips were pressed together. The face was set in an imperious sneer as the tall man glanced at the others.

Sometimes you just take an instant dislike for a man. It wasn't logical. It wasn't even good business. It made sense to think that the biggest firm, the firm with the new ships outside, would be in a position to pay the highest price.

Pat didn't always operate on logic.

"You wanta take all the fun out of it?" he asked,

grinning disarmingly at the tall, stern-faced man who represented Capcor, whatever that was.

"Are you here for fun or for a profit?" the man asked.

Pat didn't answer immediately. He noted that the clothing worn by the tall man was a sort of company uniform. Below the Capcor name and logo on the left breast pocket was the name T. O'Shields.

"These boonie rats can't match my offer," O'Shields said coldly.

"Excuse me, Mr. O'Shields," said a grizzled, thin boonie rat. "If you don't mind, I flew all night to be first in line. I have the first number." The old man sounded servile, but there was a steady gleam in his eyes as he looked at O'Shields.

"Murphy, the man isn't stupid," O'Shields said. "Your emeralds are low-grade. You can't match Capcor quality."

"Well, Mr. O'Shields," Murphy said, "I did stay up all night, so if you'll excuse me I'll let the man take a look at my stones anyhow."

Pat turned to John Hook, who was standing to one side. "Is that the usual procedure here?"

"That's it," Hook said. "First come, first bid. Then, with all bids in, the seller has the right to call for a second round of bidding if he's not satisfied."

"Murphy," O'Shields snarled, "you'll save us all valuable time if you'll just take your pebbles over to the exchange."

"And sell at Capcor prices," Murphy said.

"I think we'll observe the usual procedure, gentlemen," Pat said.

Hook moved forward. "All right. Line up by number. Stay behind the line to give each man his right of private offer."

The men moved back away from the platform. O'Shields was far back in the line, glowering, as Murphy grinned at Pat and hopped with spryness up onto the platform. He looked at the cargo manifest, held in one hand. In the other hand he carried a battered leather bag.

"Well, Mr. Murphy?" Pat asked, as Murphy placed the bag on the table in front of him.

"Capcor will offer you more in number and weight," Murphy said, speaking softly so that the waiting men would not hear.

"Well, we'll just have to see about that," Pat said.

"I hear emeralds are coming back in style in the UP," Murphy said.

"Well, the diamond is still the king of jewels," Pat said.

Murphy poured a glittering, rattling mass of uncut gemstones onto the padded table top.

"That's my lot," Murphy said. "Right at two thousand carats. All good quality."

Pat lost himself for a moment in the blood fire of a ruby, shifted his attention to an oblong green beauty of an emerald, at least one hundred carats cuttable to a stylish stone of perhaps eighty carats with chips for change.

"These are good-looking stones," he said.

"Cap," Murphy said, "I know the competition. I've got my eye on one case of happy pills. I'll tell you frankly that I can buy more on this forsaken planet with them than with all these." He swept his hand over the table to indicate the stones, misjudged, knocked a dozen stones of various sizes off onto the floor, said a curse word under his breath, bent, creakingly, to begin to pick up the stones. In his haste, he brushed a few of them under the table.

Pat, feeling sorry for the man's old, frail bones, knelt and began to help. Murphy crawled partway under the table, looked at Pat squintingly. "Sound pickups in the ceiling," he said, throwing a glance upward. "Table'll block 'em. I'll make this quick. I can't show you the stone I know you'll want most. You'll have to take my word for it. I'll deliver it to you aboard your ship tonight."

Pat reached for a stone under the table, got his head under. It wasn't beyond logic, on a totalitarian planet, for there to be listening devices in the ceiling. "I don't like the sound of that," he said.

"It will be my offense, not yours."

Murphy picked up two stones, dropped one nervously. "I want off this planet, Captain. I've got a diamond, a *diamond*, mind you. Biggest one since the Capella Glory. Half of it is yours. I don't want your drugs. Let Capcor have every damned one of them. They'll pay you the most. I just want passage out. I'll come to your ship in the dark, after midnight. You get half the diamond. I get a ride out."

"Murphy," T. O'Shields yelled, from his place toward the back of the line, "pick up your rocks and quit wasting our time."

"Why do you want off this planet so badly?" Pat asked, with the little warning bells going off in his head.

"I got just a few years left. I got me a diamond big enough so's I can enjoy 'em on a civilized planet. You get rich, too." He gathered up the last stone. "Deal?"

Pat held three emeralds in his hand. The man

had a king's ransom in gemstones if he had been on a civilized planet. He was offering them for one case of stress relievers.

"Them things are a dime a dozen on Taratwo," Murphy said, as if reading his mind. "It's the diamond, man. The diamond. It's enough for both of us."

"What would the local law have to say about you visiting me onboard ship?" Pat asked.

"It's legal," Murphy said. "They won't care about me leaving, either. Come and go as you please, but the trouble is there might not be another ship for five years."

"Mr. Murphy, I'll keep an open mind," Pat said, thinking of a huge diamond. He didn't know just how big the Capella Glory had been, but he remembered reading about it, and it was bigger than any other quality diamond found to date on any planet.

Pat wrote down Murphy's offer. The old man gathered his stones and shuffled away. The other traders filed past one by one, displaying their gems, not many of them as fine as Murphy's had been. The traders bartered without hope, fully expecting him to hand over all his cargo to the smirking O'Shields.

He was tempted to take O'Shields's offer. The Capcor man opened a fancy velvet-lined case built to carry uncut gems, displaying them to their best advantage. He did, indeed, have some beauties. Pat looked at tray after tray of uncut emeralds and rubies, and there were four small diamonds, all under one carat.

"Not too many diamonds on Tara?" he asked. Murphy's words were haunting him. Bigger than the Capella Glory? Pat's brain dredged back into

memory. The Capella Glory was still uncut. It was
on display at the Museum of Galactic Natural History on Old Earth, which was a museum planet in
itself, what with all the archaeological digs and
underwater searches which went on year after year,
century after century, as man tried, mostly in vain,
to search for his roots.

"The problem is that this is a very young planet,
and still in upheaval," O'Shields said. "You locate
a likely diamond pipe, start digging, and there's a
quake and you lose all the work you've done. A few
diamonds have been found near the surface, like
the other stones. If there are any big ones, we'll
have to find a way to dig through earthquakes to
get to them."

"Still, you have a few here," Pat said.

"Capcor is the government monopoly," O'Shields
said. "We own all the diamondiferous areas on
this planet."

Curious, Pat thought, as he tallied up all the
offers. Either the old man was lying or there was a
diamond producing pipe somewhere unknown to
Capcor.

Capcor's bid, written in the neat, precise hand of
T. O'Shields, listed sizes and weights, so that it
wasn't necessary for Pat to tabulate. He worked on
all the other offers and grinned when he saw that
by splitting the cargo into small lots, giving some
of the independent traders a share, he'd best
O'Shields offer by a few carats, even if some of the
stones were of lesser quality. He wasn't greedy.
For some reason emeralds and rubies were common on most UP planets. He wasn't going to become independently wealthy on this deal. It would
be a nice bonus, as he'd hoped, but that was all.

Too many rubies and emeralds, beautiful as they were.

But diamonds. The rarest. The king of stones.

Pat had a sudden flash of insight. T. O'Shields reminded him of his department head back at Xanthos U. That clinched it for him.

"All right, gentlemen," he called out. "I've accepted the following offers. By lot number here we are. . . ."

Before Pat could finish reading off the names, O'Shields pushed his way through the grinning, back-slapping independents. "Dammit," O'Shields sputtered. "You can call for a second round of bidding and I'll top these boonie rats."

"Where I come from," Pat said, meeting O'Shield's gaze with a smile, "an honest trader makes his top offer first time around." That was an outright lie, for all traders lived to haggle, but he didn't care if O'Shields knew it was a lie.

The knight in shining armor, soaring around the galaxy rooting for the underdog.

Pat accepted John Hook's official-sounding invitation to have lunch. The restaurant windows overlooked the not very scenic space port. The restaurant was a popular place, crowded with executive types in business dress, a few of the independent traders in their worn outdoor clothing, working-class people in neat blue uniforms.

Taratwo's women seemed to average on the skinny side, with the predominant hair colorings being shades of red and black. The men were also uniformly spare, solemn, mostly unsmiling, but then there didn't seem to be much to smile about on Tara, planet of ashes, smoke, half-light. But the green salad was tangy, the dressing good sour cream, the meat slightly tough but well flavored.

Hook's conversation between bites was banal. He hoped that the morning's trading had been profitable. Pat assured him that it had been. Hook mentioned that there was no export tax on gemstones. Pat said that was good news indeed. Without a government bite into his profits he just might be able to pay for a complete refitting of the *Skimmer*, make her more comfortable, put in a new storage capsule in the library, decontaminate the cloud chambers in the cranky computer.

Pat thought only once that afternoon of the old man. He tended to believe T. O'Shields, especially when he asked Hook about diamonds and was told that Taratwo wasn't a good diamond planet. The chances of Murphy's having a king-size diamond seemed slim. Maybe the old man was a victim of too many nights alone in Taratwo's dismal outback, a little mixed up in the head.

Pat asked Hook a few questions about local conditions, and as long as his curiosity did not touch on politics, personal freedom, or the quality of life-style he was answered. Hook's response to a sensitive question was to cough, look away, and change the subject immediately.

Pat had finished his meal and was having a taste of a very good local brandy. "Excellent," he said. "Very good."

"Grapes like a volcanic soil," Hook said.

"Make a good export, this."

Hook laughed. "First we have to make enough for local consumption."

The buzz of conversation died around them. The sudden silence was a silence of attention. Pat looked up, saw that all eyes were directed to the windows. A sleek, modern atmospace yacht was wafting down onto the largest space-port pad.

"The Man," someone at a nearby table said.

"Not likely," someone else said.

"We'll know soon enough."

"More likely the Man's redheaded friend."

"The Man's whore, you mean."

John Hook shifted nervously. He cast a glare toward the voice, then looked quickly away. The voices died into whispers. Then there was silence throughout the dining room as the port of the sleek yacht hissed open and a female figure dressed in purple skirts emerged and walked gracefully to a luxurious ground car.

"Definitely not the Man," someone said, and there was a burst of relieved, nervous laughter.

"The Leader's yacht?" Pat asked Hook.

"But not Himself. He values his privacy. He's seldom seen in public these days." He pushed himself away from the table. "My duty calls. I hope that you enjoyed your lunch."

"I did," Pat said.

"Should you wish to visit our city I have left word at the terminal to arrange transport for you," Hook said.

"Thanks, but I think I'll go back aboard. I haven't yet adjusted to Taratwo time."

The street outside the restaurant was cordoned off by lines of neatly uniformed men, tall, strong-looking men armed with the latest in sidearms. A caravan of big ground cars came blasting suddenly around the corner of the building, the lead vehicle wailing a warning. A late-model Zede executive limousine was sandwiched in between two armored police cars. As it swept past, Pat got just a glimpse of a pale, feminine face framed by fiery red hair. The Man's redheaded friend? The Man's whore?

It was none of his affair. All he wanted from Taratwo now was a passenger and a clear blink route for space.

Pat wasn't really sleepy, but he had no desire to go into the city. He stretched his legs by walking toward the passenger terminal. Inside there was dusty luxury in leather seats and wide spaces, all empty. Only one counter was manned. Pat caught the eye of the stiff-faced young man there and nodded.

"May I help you, sir?" the young man asked.

"No, no. I'm just having a bit of a walk."

"Not much to see around here, sir. If you'd like to go into the city, Captain Hook has arranged a vehicle for you."

"Very kind of him," Pat said. "But I think I'll just have a walk and go back aboard." He turned away and started out of the terminal area.

"Sir," the man behind the counter said, "it looks as if we're in for an ashfall this afternoon. I see that you don't have a breather. If you'll permit me . . ." He came out from behind the counter with a lightweight respirator unit in his hands.

"I think I can make it to the ship without that," Pat said, although the sky had darkened considerably in the short time since he'd left the restaurant.

"If you're not familiar with the effects of an ashfall you've got an unpleasant surprise coming."

Pat decided to humor the man, stood still while the mask was fitted to his face with adjustable straps. He reached for his pocket.

"Oh, no, sir," the young man said. "No charge. All visitors are furnished with breathers through the generosity of Brenden."

Brenden was the Man, the ruler.

"Tell Brenden when you see him that I thank him," Pat said.

A brief smile crossed the young man's stiff face. "That's not likely," he said. "But you're welcome to the breather. It's about the only thing that's free on this planet. Just leave it with the customs man who checks you off."

Before he reached the *Skimmer* he was glad he'd taken the mask. Ash was drifting in little windrows on the surface of the port, jetting up around his feet at each step. The decontaminator in the airlock whined and puffed getting rid of the ash which clung to his clothing and his shoes.

John Hook arrived late in the afternoon, escorted by four armed guards. By then the ashfall was so dense that although the *Skimmer*'s instruments warned him of the approach of the vehicle, he didn't see it until it was within a hundred feet of the ship. The decontaminator had to puff and whine again, and then his gemstones were aboard. Hook watched in silence as he checked the contents of the small cases.

Pat offered coffee. "I wish I had time, Captain Howe," Hook said. He turned to the armed guards who were standing by in the airlock, made a motion of dismissal. When the guards were outside, the lock closed, Hook held out his hand. "Have a pleasant trip, Captain." He leaned close. "Five a.m.," he whispered. Pat nodded. Paranoia was catching. Unless Taratwo had techs of incredible cleverness there wasn't a chance of being spied on aboard *Skimmer*, because Pat had spent a lot of money to make the ship impervious to any penetration.

Early evening seemed to be the time for earth tremors. A shock hit the space port just after darkness gave additional impenetrability to the ash fall. Pat could not even see the lights of the customs building.

A piece of nut pie made from an ancient recipe put Pat over his allowance of carbohydrates for the day, and he tried to work it off in the exercise gym. What the heck. A man had to celebrate now and then. He quit the exercise early, before he'd even worked up a sweat, and drew another ancient recipe from the nutrition servo, a concoction of gin, vermouth, and a touch of bitters. Restless, impatient, not at all sleepy, he punched up the film list. It was going to be a boring trip home, because there wasn't a film he hadn't seen at least twice.

Suddenly he had a mind picture of the redheaded Zedeian actress, and, remembering his vivid and rather erotic dream about her, punched up the film and settled back.

Corinne Tower was, he decided, as he ignored action and dialogue, the most beautiful woman he'd ever seen. Her hair was a blazing fall of lustrous glory when she let it hang to shoulder length. Her medium-heavy eyebrows merely drew attention to her emerald-green eyes.

Curious thing, the mind. Were Corinne Tower's emerald-green eyes the reason why he'd almost ignored Taratwo's fine rubies in favor of the emeralds? Had the Zedeian beauty been there, lurking in his subconscious with those glowing green eyes telling him, buy emeralds, buy emeralds?

It was going to be a long night. He didn't undress fully to get into bed, but lay there with his hands under his head watching the holographic image, dozed with Corinne Tower dominating his mind. She was a touchingly beautiful girl, giving the impression of old-fashioned vulnerability, most probably as the result of the role she was playing in the film.

He awoke to the persistent buzzing of an alarm, came into full awareness instantly, leaped to check the telltale on the panel as his adrenal glands pumped. His heartbeat decreased slowly when he realized that he was not, after all, in space, where an alarm can mean quite a number of things, not many of them pleasant. He was still on solid ground on glorious Taratwo, and the alarm had been from an outside motion detector. He activated the night-vision scanners. The ashfall had lessened. There was at least three inches of ash drifted on the tarmac, and it showed tracks. The old miner, Murphy, was standing in front of the main hatch with that same leather bag in his hand. Pat glanced at his watch. Four a.m. He'd slept a long time. His passenger was due in an hour. He'd have to make Murphy's visit a short one. He turned on the outside speaker.

"I'll be with you in a minute, Murphy," he said.

He pulled on shirt and jacket, turned off the holoprojector, and was on his way to the control bridge to open the hatch when another alarm buzzed. Something big was moving swiftly toward the *Skimmer* through the drifting ash. The cameras showed nothing, but caution told him to delay opening the hatch. He checked the screens, looking for Murphy. The old man was no longer standing before the hatch, but his footprints were clearly visible in the ash.

A blinding light caused all active cameras to show white before they could close aperture. *Skimmer* was surrounded by four armored vehicles. He flipped the armament ready switch and reached for the fire-control helmet just as a man burst into view, running from the shelter of *Skimmer*'s stern into the glare of the spotlights from the four vehicles. The running man took only a few strides before projectile weapons spat from two of the ground cars and then two more faltering, wilting steps before falling limply into the ash, sending up a small cloud.

Pat had the four vehicles targeted. One directed thought and they'd be smashed into junk. The *Skimmer*'s shield was up. It caused the hair on the head of a uniformed policeman to stand straight up as he walked to the hatch and began to pound on the hull with the butt of a weapon.

"Hull contact," the computer said aloud.

"I know, I know," Pat said.

He deliberately waited a few seconds, then opened the outside speakers. "Yeah? Who is it?" he asked, trying to make his voice sound sleepy.

"Security police, captain. There has been a slight disturbance. Please open your hatch."

Pat checked the targeting of the laser beams on the four vehicles, adjusted the fire-control helmet, walked slowly back, and opened the hatch. The security man was tall, well-built. He had holstered his weapon.

"Sorry to disturb you, sir," he said. "Port Security detected a prowler near your ship." He was trying to see past Pat. There wasn't much to see, just a bulkhead. Pat wasn't about to *invite* him in. "Were you expecting company, sir?"

Pat didn't lie. "Man, it's the middle of the night." He looked at his watch, yawned, brushed his hand through his mussed hair. The passenger was due in less than an hour and Murphy was dead, killed just for being there near the *Skimmer*. What the hell was going on? He hoped that Hook knew what he was doing. The policeman who stood in the airlock with him looked capable. He'd certainly arrived in a hurry to kill the old man.

"Your detectors did not warn you of a prowler?" the security man asked.

"Well, I didn't have them on," Pat lied. "Being here on a civilized planet ..."

The policeman's eyes did not smile with his lips. "Well, sir, I think we'd better take a look around. Taratwo is an orderly, peaceful planet, but there has been some resentment growing over the UP's high-handed actions."

This was the first Pat had heard of that. Neither X&A nor Control had indicated any anti-UP feeling on Taratwo.

"I'll join you," Pat said, acting as if he automatically assumed that the security man meant to take a look around *outside* the ship.

"Do you always wear your fire-control helmet?" the security man asked.

Pat looked him dead in the eyes. "Only when armed vehicles start shooting men around my ship," he said.

"I assume you have your laser beams aimed at my vehicles."

"Too close to the ship to use explosives," Pat said.

"You put it on the line, don't you, Captain?"

"When necessary," Pat said.

"There will be no problem."

The ashfall was finer, more pervasive in creeping into any opening in clothing. It sifted down his neck, crawled up his sleeves. He led the security man on a circuit of *Skimmer*. The officer knew his stuff; he ran his gloved hands into crevices, into the tubes of the flux drivers. Pat examined the portside thrusters, and his heart leaped as his hand contacted something soft inside a tube. He squeezed, pushed, recognized the feel of the old man's small leather bag. He could not have explained why he remained silent about the bag.

Murphy's body was being casually loaded onto one of the ground vehicles. A young security man walked up, steps puffing ash, saluted. "There is no identification on the body, sir."

"Humm," the officer said. He looked at Pat, his eyes squinted in the glare of the white spotlights. "During your trading session this morning did anyone say anything unusual to you, sir? Perhaps ask for transportation off the planet?"

"No, no," Pat said thoughtfully.

"Would you mind taking a look at the body, sir?"

"Any particular reason?"

"To see if you know the man."

"I'll do that," Pat said.

He followed the officer to the ground vehicle. The old man was heaped in a sad, slack pile on the floorboards. The officer used one gloved hand to flip Murphy onto his back and expose his face.

"I think he was one of the traders," Pat said, bending over, thinking, hell, Murphy, oh, hell. "Yes, I'm sure of it. I even remember his name. He had the first number, bought a case of stress relievers. Name's Murphy. He had some very good emeralds and rubies."

"Why do you suppose he approached your ship in the dead of night?" the officer asked.

"I have no idea," Pat said. "I've never been here before. I know no one on this planet except Captain John Hook, of customs, whom I met about thirty-six hours ago on landing. I saw this man in the customs shed during trading. I have his signature on a bill of sale for his gemstones. That's the sum total of my knowledge."

There was a moment of strained silence. Then the security officer made a slight bow. "On behalf of my government, sir, I hope you will forgive this bother."

"No big deal," Pat said. But in the back of his mind there was, surprisingly, a little prayer forming for the old man. "But do you always shoot on sight?"

"When a man is in a restricted area, and he runs from the police, he is taking his chances." The security man gave Pat a sloppy salute. "Well, good night, sir. I understand you're leaving at dawn."

"Right."

"Have a pleasant trip. I hope that you won't let this incident keep you from making a return trip to our planet soon."

"The trading is good," Pat said.

He closed the airlock, waited for decontamination. A suspicion hit him. The hatch had been open all the time he was out there with the security man. Had the whole incident been staged in order to steal his cargo of gems? He ran to the cargo area, opened one small case after the other. All the gems were there.

He sat in the command seat, a cup of coffee steaming in his hand. Well, Pat, he told himself. Thinking time. The old man had wanted off the planet very badly, badly enough to offer him half of a fabulous diamond which might or might not have existed. Now the old man was dead. May he rest in peace. And there was a small bag thrust up into the tube of a portside flux thruster. Suddenly

his hands shook. What if it was a bomb? What if
Murphy had fooled hell out of him, acting the part
of the underdog to get his sympathy in order to get
close enough to the *Skimmer* to blow her open and
get back the gems?

He had a burning urge to go outside and check
that damned bag. But the police had been able to
spot Murphy in the midst of an ashfall. That meant
they had detection instruments which were not
foiled by the ash. If he went out now and got the
bag and they were watching he'd have more to
explain than he wanted.

Twenty minutes before his passenger was due to
arrive. He activated the computer, began his pre-
takeoff countdown. He decided he wouldn't wait
until dawn if, indeed, his passenger arrived at five
a.m.

The *Skimmer* checked out beautifully. She even
told him that there was a foreign object in the
number three port thruster. The computer, fresh
after a nice rest, hummed and was brisk and efficient when he programmed the blink which would
take him away from Taratwo into orbital position.
He was ready. Five minutes to wait. He had a
leather bag containing only God knew what in a
thruster. A man had been killed before his eyes.

The flux thruster would blow the bag out, disin-
tegrating it, when he activated the engines. Unless
the bag contained an explosive triggered to ignite
with the thruster.

The motion detector buzzed. A ground car. The
air outside was becoming more clear of ash. He
picked up the vehicle at fifty yards, followed it to a
stop near the ramp, saw a small man in a baggy
white one-piece get out and walk unhurriedly toward the hatch. A quick, rather severe tremor

caused the man to stumble, and *Skimmer*'s gyros complained as the ship rocked. No police. No glaring lights. No other motion detected. Pat opened the hatch, watched on the monitor as his passenger entered the hatch carrying one small, expensive-looking bag. The ground vehicle leaped into motion and disappeared while the hatch was closing. Pat waited until the decontaminator had cleared the lock of ash and any odd and assorted bugs indigenous to Taratwo. Then he activated the radio and called, "Ground Control, *Skimmer*. I'm booked for a six a.m. take off. Any problem if I leave a bit early?"

He had to wait, picturing the controller checking with a higher authority. "No problem, *Skimmer*."

"I'll be back with you for clearance as soon as I make an outside visual," Pat said.

That was how he was going to find out what old Murphy had hidden in the thruster. Making a walkaround visual inspection of a ship before take-off had long since ceased to be standard practice. A pilot, after all, was an inferior instrument compared to the ship's sensors, but there were enough traditionalists left to make a visual inspection merely eccentric, not unusual. He nodded to the passenger in the airlock, told the small man to wait up front. The man still wore his breather, face hidden behind the mask and a floppy hat.

He left the number three portside thruster until last, jerked the bag out, tucked it under his arm. It was heavy enough to contain a bomb. He paused in the airlock, left the hatch open after setting the emergency-close mech. If the bag contained something unpleasant he would toss it out the hatch and push the emergency-close button while it was still in the air and then pray that *Skimmer*'s hull plates were strong enough.

There was no possibility, however, of throwing the bag out once he had opened it gingerly to find a solid object wrapped in a soiled piece of velvet. He had to use both hands to lift the object out of the bag.

It was ovate, almost egg-shaped. He hefted it and estimated it at plus three pounds in weight. It was, even in the rough, a thing of incredible beauty.

He was holding in his hands the single largest diamond in history, a diamond, if his weight estimate was anywhere near right, at least half a pound larger than the Capella Glory. He had checked the size of the Capella Glory in the library during his wait, and he knew that it was over eight thousand carats. The old man's stone would go over nine thousand. A man could name his own price for that stone, millions, perhaps even a billion.

And Murphy had died for it.

THREE

For a long moment, Pat Howe stood in the airlock, the hatch still open, stunned, his eyes hypnotized by the fiery depths of the diamond. Finally, he pushed the button to close the hatch and began to think again. The stone was not his. He considered his alternatives. He could call the hard-eyed security man and try to explain how the stone had come into his possession. Or he could get the hell off Taratwo and from a safe distance worry about finding the rightful owner of what just might be the most valuable single object in the civilized galaxy.

That was no choice at all. He was beginning to be just a little bit spooked. He'd been involved in more than one hairy situation during his relatively brief career in free enterprise. Once he'd played a deadly game of hide-and-seek on an airless moon with his air running out and two men intent on killing him. Once he'd had to run for his life after he'd lifted the ransom loot from a Hogg Moons pirate, the kidnap victim clinging to him, slowing him down. And the total amount of money at stake in both those incidents wouldn't buy a cutting chip from the diamond he held in his hands. Men had killed for a tiny fraction of the worth of that diamond, and even a man who had never entertained a criminal thought might be tempted toward murder by something so valuable.

He left the diamond, in its bag, with the other gems in cargo, ran to the bridge, and wondered what had happened to his passenger. The passenger would be housed in the spare cabin. It was crowded, for he used it to store items used only occasionally, but the bed was as large and as comfortable as his own. He jerked the door open to find the room empty.

There were not many places aboard *Skimmer* where a man could hide. He didn't like the idea of his passenger wandering around down in the engine room, so he decided to check his own quarters first. The lock on the door had gone bad on the trip out and he hadn't bothered to fix it. He threw the door open.

She stood beside his bed, the white one-piece at her feet, breather and hat removed to show a fall of lustrous auburn hair, slightly mussed but still glorious. Her skin was the pale hue of old china. She wore only a tight, brief silken camiknicker, blue.

"Sorry," he said, starting to close the door. The shock was slow to penetrate. A woman. And not just any woman. It was as if the holographic image had come to life, full-sized and breathing, in his cabin.

She reached for a garment she'd removed from her bag, not in haste or modesty. "I assumed this would be my cabin," she said, with a smile which matched the blaze of her hair. "I also assumed that you would knock before entering."

Corinne Tower. His passenger was Corinne Tower, the film star from Zede II, and she was not at all discomfited as she stood there in a silken piece of underwear which emphasized her perfect figure. She seemed to flow into a wraparound which closed off the view of womanly curves. Her smile had faded into a musing expression.

Pat was paralyzed until the buzz of an alarm jerked his head around, and then he was on the run, the redheaded woman following him more slowly. Four police vehicles were approaching at different angles to surround the ship. There was, as yet, no light of dawn. The ashfall had diminished almost to nothing. The night-vision cameras showed clearly that the police vehicles had uncovered their weapons. Pat's hand slapped switches, buttons. Shield up, weapons ready. The lead vehicle mounted a respectable laser cannon with a long, graceful barrel. Up close, it could punch a hole in *Skimmer*'s shield *and* hull.

"Should we be worried about this?" he asked the girl.

She was taut, her mouth open, eyes narrowed. "I'm not sure."

"Did the Man know you planned to leave?" Her eyes instantly shifted away from his.

"Quickly," he said, his voice urgent. "I'm going to have to rely on your knowledge and judgment. I don't want to do anything drastic unless it's necessary."

She seemed doubtful. "He was in the outback. Not due back until tomorrow."

The lead vehicle had come to a halt, cannon pointed toward *Skimmer*'s weakest point, the main entry hatch. The same tall, efficient security man who had visited him only a short time before was standing behind the laser cannon. Pat activated the outside pickups.

"You have just ten seconds to open, Captain, and then we'll blast you open."

He couldn't wait for more information from the girl. "Wake up, old man," he told the computer. The blink was already programmed, but it was customary for a ship to lift from the surface on flux. It was possible to blink away from a planet's surface, but decidedly unsafe for anything near enough to the ship to be affected by the field of the blink generator.

The policeman was counting, ". . . six, five . . ."

"Let's go, baby," Pat said, hitting the button which activated the drive circuits.

". . . three, two . . ."

There was a brief, uneasy slide into nothingness. On the screen Pat saw three of the police vehicles tumbling in free space. They'd been too near the ship. They'd been enclosed in *Skimmer*'s powerful field, and now men were dying of explosive decompression in the vacuum of space. A body, bursting as he watched, separated itself from a vehicle and spun slowly, eerie things happening to frail flesh and blood. It was the security officer.

"Oh, my God," Corinne Tower whispered as an alarm screamed, sending Pat into motion. Two Taratwo light cruisers were closing rapidly. His screen was up. He jerked the fire-control helmet onto his head, wondering how the hell the cruisers had known to be there. True, a blinking ship sends a signal ahead of itself into space, pointing to the emergence site, but the cruisers would have had to be ready to blink instantly, would have had to be watching him in order to detect that preblink signal.

Gun ports began to flare on the closing warships. Lasers. Two sleek and deadly ship-to-ship missiles swam out as if in slow motion from the lead cruiser and then accelerated with slashes of light. Range seven miles. Seconds. No time to program a blink. The lead missile was growing rapidly on the screen as the ship buzzed and screamed warnings.

"Alert, alert," the computer chanted, losing, for the moment, its reluctance for audio communication.

"I hear you," Pat said, forgetting the presence of the tense, silent girl.

He had only one advantage. He couldn't hope to match shields and armaments with two new cruisers, but he had power to spare, power built into the old space tug, power to latch on to and haul the biggest space liner ever built, the generator built oversize, huge enough to store power for multiple blinks without draining the charge. He had used only a small portion of the charge in blinking up from the surface of Taratwo.

No time to select known coordinates. No time to trust a cranky, aging computer to obey a vocal order to select a registered blink beacon at random and put it in B for boogie. The old boy might decide to take a full survey of all blink beacons within range.

He acted on his only choice.

In spite of what Jeanny Thompson, and others, might have thought, Pat Howe was not like some old-fashioned mercenaries, imbued with a secret death wish, seeking danger for the thrill of risking it, courting the final solution, death, as ordinary men court women. Pat valued his freedom, and he valued his life. He did what he had to do to preserve that life with two homing missiles inches away from his thrusters, heading in, and two light cruisers tickling *Skimmer*'s shield with laser cannon. Either of the cruisers could best him in a close-in fight, and there was no question in his mind that their intent was to blast him out of space.

The computer was cranky. The missiles should have been taken out by AMMs before they were allowed to get in so close. At the last moment the old man sent out the hunter-killer AMMs, and the resultant explosions were far too close to the hull, but there was no new blare of noise from the alarms to indicate hull rupture, only a wild ride for a moment, and then Pat's fingers stabbed once, twice, three times and there was that sliding feeling of blinking and he was still alive and breathing after doing the most dangerous thing a spaceman could do, take a wild blink.

Taking a random blink was recklessly dangerous because astronomical bodies ranging in size down to the tiniest asteroids were deadly hazards. Two bodies cannot exist at the same point in space and time. A ship, passing through that nowhere which is a blink, would merge, down to the molecular level, with any object already occupying a point in space and time on the chosen route, the result being instant death for any life form.

Pat had gambled and he'd won. He had set coordinates in no conscious order. It gave him, however, only a few seconds respite, for the Taratwo cruisers were equipped with the latest in follow-and-detect equipment, and there they were, within ten miles of the *Skimmer*, and they loosed a cloud of missiles, leaped into motion to close the range. Pat had to stay ahead of them. It was obvious now that they were equipped with the new multiblink generators. There were so many missiles coming that he didn't have enough AMMs to stop them. His fingers jabbed figures off the top of his head into the computer.

The children of Old Earth had brought into space with them the legend of a deadly, ancient game played with an antique projectile weapon with six chambers for explosive-driven bullets. Pat's game was like that ancient one. He had pulled the trigger once and the firing pin had fallen on an empty chamber. He pulled the trigger a second time, held his breath through the blink slide, lived, and the two cruisers were right behind him.

He fired his own missiles, hating to do it. The damned things were the latest Zedeian technology and they cost a mint, but it would give him seconds while the cruisers put out their own AMMs to wipe out his total missile armament. Surely, considering the value of space aboard a ship of the line, the cruisers wouldn't be able to follow still another multiblink without recharging. But he'd won a deadly gamble twice. He didn't dare try it a third time. With the few seconds he'd bought with his six missiles, he told the computer to pick the nearest blink beacon and go.

"Arrrr," he growled, the sound becoming a moan as the old man began to make a total survey of all blink beacons within ten parsecs. An alarm screamed, telling him that the shield had taken a direct laser hit. The screen gave off an odd aroma of strain and heat. He'd had that scent in his nose only once before, when he was playing dodge-'em with that pirate ship out near the Hogg Moons. His instruments told him that the power of the shield was already down, expended in absorbing the close, direct blaze of the cannon.

So, with a silent prayer, he pulled the trigger and came out close to a blazing sun, a very near thing, and now more alarms clanged, telling him of too much heat, too much radiation in the solar wind from the star which filled his viewscreens. He considered kicking in the flux drive, but that would take too long. By the time he gained safe distance from the star the entire hull would be radioactive. He punched in a very, very short blink, a relatively safe blink, just to the limit of his optical scanners, and he disappeared just as the two cruisers emerged. This time he had empty space around him, after his fourth random blink, the last one less risky than the first three. He put the *Skimmer* on flux to get him away from the point of emergence. The fact that the two Taratwo cruisers hadn't followed immediately indicated that they'd have to charge their generators before blinking again, and by that time the flux drive would have put him beyond the range of their sensors. He could take his time finding a blink beacon and make one more leap before he had to recharge *Skimmer*'s generator. He wasn't about to try for a fifth empty chamber in the gun.

Corinne Tower had stood quietly by. From the tense look on her face he guessed that she had realized the danger of the random blinks. He set the computer to work. This time the old boy had reason to begin a 360-degree map. Pat didn't see a single familiar feature anywhere in space. The very shape of the disk of the galaxy had rotated, altering the appearance of the dense star clouds toward the core.

Random blinks are dangerous in more ways than one. There is no theoretical limit to the distance covered by a blinking ship. The only limitation to the length of a blink is a known, straight-line distance between two previously determined points, the distance being free of solid objects. In punching in random numbers, Pat had chosen numbers in the range of known blink coordinates, but that didn't guarantee anything. He could be anywhere within ten parsecs or a thousand parsecs of Taratwo. Or, if his fingers had picked a rather funny number in his haste, *Skimmer* could be drifting along silently on the flux drive in an entirely different galaxy.

He left the computer to do its valiant duty and turned to face the woman. He wiped perspiration from his forehead.

"Four random blinks?" she asked. He nodded grimly.

"Bad computer?"

"Not bad," he said. "Just cranky and slow."

"So you have no idea where we are," she said.

"Not a clue."

She sighed. "Is there anything I can do?"

Suddenly he was very tired. He checked the computer. The old man was muttering to himself, building the maps steadily, cross-checking against all the charts of the galaxy.

"Yes," Pat said. "You can move your things out of my quarters. Put them in the mate's quarters." He pointed to the door. "And then I think you and I had better have a talk." He wanted to hit the sack, rest, sink into sleep while the computer puttered over the maps. It might take hours if they were far from known blink routes.

At first an odd expression had crossed her face, then she smiled. "I'm sorry," she said. "I didn't notice that the alarms and remotes were in that cabin."

He could have explained that, instead of merely ordering her out of his quarters, but he wasn't in a very polite mood.

"And," she said, "I guess I owe you that talk." She turned gracefully, started toward his cabin. The garment showed the litheness of her legs, the rounded perfection of her. He sat down in the command chair, punched up coffee. She emerged carrying her bag, put it in the mate's cabin, came to sit on the bench facing him.

"How do you take it?" he asked, pointing his mug at her.

"Strong and black," she said with a smile. In real life her smile was even more impressive than in holograph. He felt the anger and tension begin to fade out of him.

"All right," he said, as he handed her her mug. "I was told that you would be a perfectly legal passenger, that there'd be no hassle getting you off Taratwo. We seem to be in the clear now, but I would like to know, since I'm rather attached to this ship and its main cargo, me, if I can expect any more surprises."

Her emerald eyes narrowed thoughtfully, and she worried her lower lip with her perfect teeth for a moment. "I suppose the cruisers can follow us to the point of emergence of the last blink."

"Let me worry about the technicalities," he said, his voice unnecessarily brusque. "What I want to know is why they came after us and if we can, possibly, expect them to make another try, perhaps with knowledge of our destination so that they can intercept us as we come onto the charted blink routes leading to Zede II."

"I don't think they'd dare use force in UP space," she said.

"You're not being very informative," he said.

"I don't know why," she said. Her voice was full, vibrant.

"The Man didn't want you to leave?"

"He was away, in the outback."

"But he was, ah, fond of you?"

She smiled broadly. "Quite," she said.

He realized that to get any information out of her he was going to have to be persistent. "Why were you on Taratwo?"

Was that a quick look of relief which crossed her face? "Brenden is a very good customer of the Zedeian conglomerate which produces my pictures," she said. "He was a great fan. He kept asking that I be sent out to Taratwo on a publicity tour, and apparently his arms business was desirable enough that my producer put pressure on me to go."

Pat felt revulsion. "So you went," he said flatly. "There were no other producers of pictures in the galaxy, so you obeyed." He had dirty little pictures of his own running through his mind.

Her eyes hardened as she stared directly at him. "I made public appearances in the major cities, and I was a guest in Brenden's manor house. I enjoy my work, but I don't prostitute myself for it."

"Sorry," he said, thinking, yeah, yeah. "I'm just trying for a scenario to explain why Brenden's men were willing to kill rather than let you go."

"It doesn't occur to you that it was you they were trying to stop?"

"Hey, no sale on that idea. I'm just a free trader. They had no reason to want to stop me. If they'd wanted to take back the gemstones I traded for they had a perfect opportunity before you boarded."

"Oh?" she asked.

So why was he the one who was giving out information? He grinned at himself. He wanted to believe her, believe that she had not been, as the men said in the space port's restaurant, Brenden's whore. She was, by far, the most beautiful woman he'd ever seen, and he was going to be alone with her on *Skimmer* for a couple of weeks.

"The security police killed a man who was prowling around my ship," he said.

Her hand went to her lips and her eyes widened. "Oh, no," she said. "I—" Then she recovered quickly.

"You know something about that? Did you know an old man named Murphy?"

"Poor John," she whispered. "They killed him?"

"Very, very dead."

"But you have the diamond. I watched on the screens as you took Murphy's bag out of a thruster tube."

Pat tried to hide his surprise by lifting his coffee cup, hiding behind it for a moment, taking too big a gulp so that it burned his mouth.

"He wasn't lying to you," she said. "We were going to give you half."

"We?" he asked.

"All right," she said. "I guess it's time to put it all up front and be honest."

"I'd deeply appreciate that," he said.

"Murphy knew that I'd be leaving Taratwo. He got my attention by sending me dozens of expensive bouquets, adoring fan letters, and finally I agreed to see him. He had the diamond right there with him in that same leather bag. He said that if the government or the government gem monopoly found out that he had it they'd take it from him.

I felt sorry for him. He'd spent his life on various out-planets and that was his first big strike. He almost lost his life getting it, digging a diamond pipe that was quite near an active volcano, always in danger of being buried alive by an earthquake collapsing his shaft. I guess I'm soft, but I thought he should enjoy the fruits of his luck and labor. I told him I'd help, notify him when I was leaving, arrange a sale for the diamond when we were back on Zede II."

"You didn't have to help much," Pat said. "He did it all himself, contacted me, came to the ship himself."

"But I told him about you, told him when you would arrive and when you'd be leaving." A small tear came to her right eye and fell, rolling down her cheek. "I thought he was aboard, hiding. I kept waiting for you to tell me that there was another passenger."

"But you, you and Murphy, were going to give me half of the sales value? How much was in it for you?"

Her lips tensed in quick anger, then she shook her head. "Well, I don't really blame you for thinking that."

"So what do we do now? Do we split it fifty-fifty?" He didn't know why, but there was something in him that seemed to be driving him to be harsh with her when what he wanted to do was exactly 180 degrees away from harshness.

She drew herself up proudly. "If that's the way you want it."

"We might wonder if Murphy had children, a wife back in the UP somewhere," Pat said.

"Oh? And you'd be generous and honorable and give the diamond to them?"

"Would you?"

She rose and walked away, and when she spoke, her face turned away from him, her voice was strained. "You won't believe it, I'm sure, but that's exactly what I would do. As it happens, however, he was alone, no close kin, an old man who wanted only to spend his last years in comfort on some nice planet."

He wanted to go to her, put his arms around her, tell her that he was sorry. "Hey," he said. "OK. I'm sorry. I believe you would do that. I didn't know the old man well, but I'm sorry he's dead." She turned to face him. The computer was purring and clicking as it built a nice, three-dimensional map on the screens, working with smooth efficiency to find one, just one, point of reference.

"Could the security police have been after the diamond?" he asked.

"I don't think so. I don't see how they could have known."

"They had to have a reason. If not the diamond, you. Maybe Brenden wasn't ready for you to leave."

"He wouldn't have tried to kill me," she said, her voice strong, sure.

"All right. It's going to take the old man a while to get a fix. Are you hungry?" She nodded with almost childish eagerness. "Care to check the menu, or shall I just give you *Skimmer*'s best?"

"Please," she said, coming to sit on the padded bench again.

Skimmer wasn't a luxury liner. They ate on the bridge, and as they ate, she demonstrated that she had people skills, diverting his questions with charmingly asked questions of her own, drawing Pat out of his shell of suspicion. He found himself talking his head off, telling her about his youthful love of words and languages, of his pride at being given the chair at Xanthos University which had been endowed by the man who had first translated the one alien language which man had encountered. She was familiar with the sad, frightening story of the Artunee civilization, the story of Miaree. She had, in fact, played the part of Miaree in a Zedeian production of the tale.

"I want a copy of that," he said. "I think you'd look great with Artunee wings and those cute little antennae coming out of your forehead."

"And I'll bet you charmed all the coeds at Xanthos U," she said, turning the conversation again. "Audrey Patricia Howe." She was reading from the ship's license, mounted over the console.

Pat rolled his eyes. "You're asking?"

"Shouldn't I?"

"My mother was a certified nut."

"Poor baby," she said, pursing her lips.

"No, really, Audrey is an old family name. Mother's grandfather, Fleet Admiral Alexander P. Audrey." He rose and programmed a course change. The ship was still moving along at a small fraction of the speed of light on flux thrusters. Somewhere back there were two well-armed light cruisers, and he was making it as difficult as possible for them to track him. "Her name was Patricia, and she wanted a girl."

"Cruel," she said. "You had fights in first school because other boys teased you."

"Had to learn to fight."

"Do you also always fight with ladies?" She was swamping him, foundering him, with those green eyes. All of her attention was focused on him, on his face, his eyes.

"The last thing I want to do with you is fight," he said, smiling.

"Good." When she smiled her mouth seemed to double in size, a true east-west smile, a glory of a smile which changed every aspect of her lovely face, made her look quite young. "How long do you estimate before the computer locates us?"

He shrugged. "The old man has already gone through a few hundred possibilities, using a gradually increasing data base."

"Sorry, I'm just an actress. I don't understand that technical talk."

"Well, he builds a model of the visible star fields, then rotates the model, trying to match the stars with a known point of reference. For example, if you looked up at the night sky and saw the Bell constellation, you'd know that you were looking into space from the area of Zede II. If you were a few parsecs away from Zede II, at right angles from the plane of the Bell as seen from the planet, the Bell would be unrecognizable. Build a holo model and rotate it and soon you'd see the Bell, and from that known position, in the area of Zede II, you could figure out where you were.

"It's as clear as a Taratwo ashfall," she said, laughing.

"The computer starts with a few stars in the model, and then begins to add in more and more when rotation fails to produce any known patterns. With millions of stars to work with, he might have to construct quite a few models before he hits pay dirt."

"So we could be here for a few days?"

"Or weeks."

"We'll just have to find a way to entertain ourselves, won't we?" she asked, then she flushed hotly as he grinned.

"I won't make the obvious suggestion," he said.

"Please don't."

Not yet, he was thinking. Not yet.

For the next meal she tried her hand at making up a menu, learning the operation of the nutrition servo quickly. She went through the *Skimmer*'s film library, picked out a few of her old favorites, and with her comments, her inside knowledge of filmmaking, the often-seen pictures took on new interest for Pat.

On the third ship's day, he kissed her. Her mouth tasted of lipstick and cherries. It was just after the evening meal, and he kissed her without preliminary, rising and lifting her from the padded bench into his arms. Her mouth went soft and pliant and her arms tightened around him, and when he looked into her face she was weeping quietly, the tears welling up in those huge, blazing green eyes to wet her lashes and slip silently down onto her cheeks.

"That bad?" he asked, his voice husky with desire, which had been building, building, building.

"Please don't," she whispered.

He drew her to him again and lost himself in the glory of the feel of her, the warmth of her.

"Please don't," she repeated.

What the hell? Even though she was a Zedeian, that business of saying yes yes with the lips and no no with the tongue was passé. A woman did, or she didn't, and it was her choice, and, although the old morality was strong, the family unit the basic building block of civilization, women had long since been free, as men were, to do as they pleased.

"You're confusing me," he said, leaning toward her lips again.

"You're a nice man—"

"Just nice?"

"Please, Pat."

He released her with a sigh. "All right," he said.

"Oh," she said, in a small, hurt way.

The old man was chuckling, enjoying the demanding work, building ever more complex and complete models. Pat glanced at the screen and saw a solid glow, a mass of millions of stars, in the model now, so closely packed as to be indistinguishable from the overall mass of brightness.

"I could get very serious about you," he whispered, and felt a small shock, realizing that even though he'd made a statement which, on the surface, was not binding, he'd made a commitment.

Pat, my boy, he told himself, you've gone and done it. You're in love with this one.

"Pat, listen to me," she said.

"I'm not sure I want to. I don't think I want to hear what you're going to say."

"I can't. I just can't. I can't have that complication in my life right now. Please understand."

"Give me something *to* understand."

"I want to go to bed with you," she said, not looking at him.

"That's what I want."

"But not like this. Not so casually, just as if we *have* to because we're alone, lost in space, time on our hands."

"What better time?"

"When you're sure. When we're back home on Zede II."

"I'm sure."

"Pat, there's time."

"I have a preliminary three-point identification," the old man said, in his slightly mechanical voice.

"Great timing," Pat said.

Corinne looked at him inquiringly.

"It'll take a few minutes for him to cross-check," Pat said.

"Then we'll be going home?"

"Yes."

She came to him, lifting herself high on tiptoes, kissed him quickly. "Pat, let's talk when we're back home."

"Yeah, OK," Pat said. "I know when I'm being rejected."

"No. You're not being rejected. Please. I enjoy every minute with you, Pat. I think I'm falling in love with you, but I must be sure." She turned away. "Please understand. I've never made a commitment, not with anyone."

He felt his heart race. He wanted to believe.

"I don't want to commit under these emotional circumstances, relief at our escape from death, being alone, lost in space. Humor me?"

"Do I have a choice?"

She turned to face him. "Yes. I'll give you the choice. After all, I'm indebted to you. If you want—"

Oh, hell, he thought. That tore it. Now she was telling him she'd sleep with him out of gratitude.

A small bell rang and the computer lit up green with pride. "Position location," he said. "Position location."

"I hear you," Pat said. He took Corinne's hands in his. "OK, the old man has found us and we can be off for Zede II. I'm going to play it your way. You said you think you are falling in love with me. OK. I think I'm falling in love with you. I won't push. I'll just pester you night and day when we're back on Zede II until we're both sure."

"Deal," she said. "Let's drink to it."

He punched up her favorite, a mild, tasty fruit thing developed by a bartender whose mother must have been frightened by a fruit wagon. He had Tigian brandy. As he handed Corinne her glass she seemed to stumble, and the contents of the glass spilled onto the deck. He grabbed for a towel, bent to clean up the spill, then drew her another as she apologized for her clumsiness. He killed his brandy in two gulps, wondering why the damned computer had to pick *this* time to be efficient and quick.

He checked the charge in the blink generator. Full. Ran a security check of the *Skimmer*. All systems were perfect. He made the rounds. The generator room was prickly with charge, causing his hair to want to stand up, the huge generator giving out a sense of being almost alive.

He stumbled going back to the bridge, felt an odd sensation at the base of his skull, shook his head to dispel a feeling of dizziness. The computer had pinpointed the nearest blink route and had the coordinates for a beacon at the ready.

"Off we go," he said, as the ship blinked and the feeling of sliding merged with the dizziness in his head and blackness rushed at him from a far, glaring horizon to enfold him. A battle line of warships rushed out of the darkness, cannon blazing, and he tried to yell a warning, his hand reaching for the fire-control helmet as he fell.

There were times when he felt as if he existed in a vacuum, all blankness and darkness and not one feature for the eyes, ears, touch to discover, and then wild, frightful, nightmarish things came at him from all directions with deadly intent as he tried to scream and run in a medium which clung, held back, swallowed. Once or twice he felt warmth, soft hands on his forehead. He saw Corinne as she appeared in the film, in period costume, and she was alternately welcoming him and rejecting him. And there were strange suns with square planets peopled by the monsters of his childhood nightmares and sweet fields of wild flowers scented with Corinne's perfume, and once a big, ancient derelict of a starship alone in black space with the nearby star fields close and glowing.

Corinne, in his fevered, tossing delirium, leaned over him, whispering his name as she held a cup of soup to his lips.

"Corinne?" he croaked, having to struggle to find enough voice to say that one word.

"It's all right," she said. "Drink this."

"Corinne?"

"Yes, I'm here."

"What—happened?"

"Ah," she said, and her hand on his forehead was very, very real. "I do think you're back with us."

"Sick?"

"Very," she said. "You've been very, very ill. I think you must have picked up mindheat fever on Taratwo."

"Gggggg," he said, trying to say something that he forgot as blackness came again.

The next time he came alive he stayed awake longer. She fed him chunky things with a spoon, and he chewed, not being able to taste, but knowing he needed food.

"How long?" he croaked.

"Five days."

"That long?"

"It's rarely fatal, but sometimes the victim wishes it was."

"Where—"

"You passed out as we blinked onto the route the computer discovered. We're standing by the blink beacon."

"Got to get—" He tried to raise himself and fell back weakly. It was two more days before he could get out of bed and totter, a thousand years old, to the bridge. The computer had the route worked out. He took the ship through five blinks before he had to go back to bed to rest.

Corinne nursed him lovingly. She forced him to eat, to drink liquids. Gradually, as he guided the ship back onto more heavily traveled blink routes, each jump putting them closer and closer to Zede II, he began to get his strength back. He wouldn't have to worry about exercise. He'd lost fifteen pounds.

They orbited Zede II, and he checked into Control. There was a wait of one hour for Zede City Space Port.

"There is one thing," Corinne said.

"There are a lot of things," he said. "I'll need a place to stay, near you, so that I can see you often."

"The diamond," she said.

"What about it?"

"If you don't object, I'll keep it in my possession."

He loved her. But he was the trader. He knew that the best place to market that hunk of glory was on Xanthos, richest of the planets, center of the UP. The museums of the UP would vie with each other, bidding against private interests. "I can get a better price," he said.

"All right," she said.

"I'll find a place to stay. I'll need your address and number."

She wrote on a note pad, tore off the sheet, handed it to him. Zede Control plugged into *Skimmer's* computer, and the old man gave a warning. "Here we go down," Pat said. "When can I see you?"

"Call me tomorrow." It was morning, Zede City time.

"Why not tonight?"

"I'll have to report in," she said. "Bring the brass up to date on my tour of Taratwo."

"Tomorrow morning, first thing," he said.

"You'll have business, too, getting your money."

"Yep. Look, *Skimmer* needs an overhaul. I've been thinking of combining the two cabins. Make one big, luxurious cabin. Good place for a honeymoon."

She smiled. "I think it would be."

"Any place in the known galaxy you've always wanted to go?"

"Selbelle III, the planet of artists."

"Selbelle III it is," he said. "Do you think a week will be too long to wait to get married?"

She laughed. "You can't get *Skimmer* overhauled in a week."

They had talked. She didn't want to give up her career. He had no objections. He thought it might be fun to dabble in filmmaking. The proceeds of the sale of the diamond, which he'd tagged in his mind with the name Murphy's Stone, would make them very, very wealthy. They could produce their own films, on any civilized planet, starring Corinne Howe, or Corinne Tower if she thought it best to keep her own professional name.

"Take *Skimmer* back to Xanthos. Get her all

dolled up and clear up the old man's memory chambers. I have some loose ends to take care of here. Call me when *Skimmer*'s ready."

"I'll call every night."

"At interstellar blink rates?"

"Well."

She kissed him, hard, as the ship settled down onto the assigned pad at Zede City Space Port. "Pat, I'll be waiting," she whispered. "One thing . . ."

"When you say one thing I get nervous."

"Don't call me while you're here. Not just yet. I'm going to have to break my contract with Zedefilms. I don't need any complications. I'll be thinking of you. I'll be ready to go with you when *Skimmer*'s ready."

He stood in the airlock and watched her walk away, carrying her small bag. She walked with brisk, purposeful, and yet very graceful strides, and there were two "businessmen" in tailored suits waiting for her at the gate. A third "businessman" walked to the *Skimmer* and asked permission to come aboard. He gave Pat the interbank notice that the balance of Pat's commission had been transferred to his account.

"I understand you had some trouble with the Taratwo navy," the businessman said.

"Glad you mentioned that," Pat said. "I was told that there'd be no rough stuff, that Corinne was making a legal exit from the planet."

"The dictator fell in love with her," the man said. He shrugged. "Power-mad. We owe you a debt, Captain Howe, for getting our star safely home. If you'll take a closer look at that transfer you'll see."

A healthy bonus had been added. Hell, it was all over now, the hassle out there on that earthquake-tortured planet. And in a month or six weeks, he'd be coming back to Zede II to pick up a bride.

He spent the night in a spacers' hotel, luxuriating in a full-sized shower, good Zedeian food and drink, and a huge circular bed in which he felt almost lost but decidedly comfortable. For one brief moment he was tempted to find company. All he had to do was dial the desk. But in a month or six weeks he'd have all the company he needed—Corinne.

He kept his promise. He didn't call. He lifted ship just after dawn and was soon back on Xanthos, traveling quickly down well-populated blink routes. *Skimmer* was moved to a pad in the repair yards. Pat offloaded the gems, being especially careful with Murphy's leather bag. He locked the diamond, still in the leather bag, in his office safe, made an excursion to the gem markets, and came back with his bank account well fortified, for the price of emeralds was up. It was time to show Murphy's Stone to a few selected people, but before he made the first call he opened the safe and took out Murphy's bag. His mind was telling him that the diamond couldn't be as large as he remembered it.

He put the bag on his desk, opened it, pulled away the soiled velvet wrap, and froze in place. Where there should have been a huge, gleaming uncut diamond there was foil wrapping. He began to jerk and tear at the foil and uncovered a mass of small metal tools and parts obviously taken from *Skimmer*'s stores. The metal, just over three pounds' worth, was encased in storage gel molded to match the shape of Murphy's Stone.

He was on the communicator within seconds. It took a few minutes to get through to Zede II. He gave the Zede City operator Corinne's number, wondering what time it was on Zede II.

"I'm sorry, sir, the number you have given me is not an operating number."

"Check again," he said.

There was not and had never been such a number in Zede City. The address she'd given him was that of a ground-car salesroom in Zede City's business section. He was a bit more than irate, for his anger was feeding on fear of loss, on a sense of betrayal, on a growing sadness to think that he'd lost her without even knowing why. He reached the number of the businessmen who had hired him to go out to Taratwo immediately and recognized the voice of the spokesman who had come to Xanthos to hire him.

"Ah, Captain Howe. We've been expecting your call."

"I want to be put in touch with Corinne Tower," he said.

"That is impossible now and it will be in any conceivable future."

"Dammit," he began.

"Captain Howe," the smooth Zedeian voice said, "you were paid well to perform an errand. You did very well. You came briefly into possession of an object to which you have no claim. Nor do you have any claim on Corinne Tower. Take your profit, Captain, and go about your business. If we ever need your services again, you can be sure we'll pay well, but, as the old saying goes, don't call us, we'll call you. And please, to save us all problems, do not try to contact Corinne Tower."

"I'll have to hear that from her," Pat said. "You may hold a film contract on her, but you don't control her private life."

"That, too, has been anticipated," the Zedeian said. "Listen."

"Pat," Corinne's voice said, full and throaty. "I'm sorry it had to be this way. I told you I could not have complications in my life. Don't try to call me or come to see me. As for a certain object, you'll realize that you never had any right to it. That's all. Thank you for an eventful journey home."

"Is that clear enough for you, Captain Howe?" the Zedeian asked.

"I was promised half the value of that object," Pat said, not really caring about the money, or the diamond. He felt as if he'd been slugged in the belly by a giant. He hurt. He wanted to throw the communicator out the window.

"Come now," the Zedeian laughed. "Grow up, Captain Howe."

Pat hung up. "Ah, Corinne," he said.

He'd go to Zede II and find her. She'd have to tell him to his face. He was reaching for the communicator to call the space port's passenger service when it sang out a summons to him.

"Captain Audrey Patricia Howe?"

"Don't call me Audrey Patricia," he growled, recognizing Jeanny Thompson's voice.

"I'm using your title and full name because this is an official call," Jeanny said. "You're in trouble, Pat."

"What's up?" he asked. He wasn't concentrating. The reaction was setting in. Hell, he'd been crazy to think that the most beautiful woman in the world could fall for him.

"Pat, a very grim-faced officer from Xanthos Central is in my office at this moment. He has a copy of the route and travel tapes from your *Skimmer* with him."

"Why?" Pat asked. It was routine for the computer to feed the travel information to Xanthos Central Control at the end of a trip. "Did the old man goof up?" Pat asked.

"It's no computer goof, Pat," Jeanny said. "You know that it's against regulations to tamper with the automatic computer log which records the routes traveled. Of course you do. So why the hell did you erase a portion of the tape, and very clumsily at that?"

Gulp. "You're kidding."

"Pat, you'd better get over here right away. You know this is a license-lifting offense. What the hell were you thinking about?"

"Why did Central come to you?" Pat asked, stalling for time as he tried to sort out his confused thoughts. He knew that he hadn't erased the route tape.

"Because X&A is the enforcement agency, chum. It's up to us to see that dumbos who erase the route tape never take a ship into space again."

"My God, Jeanny," he said.

"You'd better get over here right away."

"Yeah, sure. Look, I'd like to go by the ship, check this out myself."

"You do that. But be in my office no later than three hours from now."

"Yes, ma'am," Pat said.

Maybe it was just the computer. The old man had been ailing, cranky. He'd have a talk with that gentleman, get to the bottom of it. But as he hurried out of his office a feeling of deep, agonizing depression hit him. What was the use? His world had been compressed into the twin green eyes of a girl. So what if X&A grounded him? What did it matter?

FOUR

A smart little flux-drive runabout with X&A marking sat directly in front of the pad on which *Skimmer* squatted, her hull showing the dullness of a long time in space, the thousand-parsec syndrome, it was called. When Pat left his vehicle and walked onto the pad a uniformed security guard blocked his way to *Skimmer*'s hatch.

"Sorry, friend," the security guard said. "This crate has been impounded by X&A."

Jeanny Thompson's pert face appeared in the open hatch. "It's all right, guard. Please let the gentleman pass."

"You've already seized the ship?" Pat asked, as he followed Jeanny onto *Skimmer*'s bridge.

"No, final seizure will take court action. Meanwhile, we're just making sure that no one comes aboard and destroys evidence."

"Jeanny, you know I didn't erase the tape," he said.

She turned to face him. "Someone did."

Corinne. He had been ill for days. Had she tried to use the computer? There were, of course, safeguards against erasing the trip log. It would take an intimate knowledge of computers or some accident against which the odds were astronomical to tamper with that separate chamber in the old man's storage areas where the trip information was recorded.

"Well?" Jeanny demanded.

"Jeanny, let me talk to the old man for a few minutes."

"I'm on your side," Jeanny said, "but I'm not about to put myself in a sling, Pat. I'm going to be looking over your shoulder. I see you trying to tamper and I call the guard."

"OK, OK," he said testily, seating himself at the old man's console. He punched up the trip tape and checked coordinates with his own handwritten log.

"Holy—" Jeanny said unbelievingly, as the four random blinks outbound from Taratwo showed on the star map which the computer was laying out on the screen. "What in the holy hell were you doing, Pat? Four random blinks?"

"I had two hostile light cruisers with all the latest armament on my tail," Pat said. "There's no law against random blinks."

"There should be a law against stupidity," she said.

The map built smoothly to record the course changes Pat had made on flux and on the blink *Skimmer* had made to get back onto an established blink route.

"Coming up," Jeanny said.

You had to be watching closely. The map showed the next blink down the range toward UP space, but there was, before that blink, just a tiny glitch, a sort of instantaneous glimmer on the screen. Pat backed up the tape and ran it again.

"That's where the delete button was pushed," Jeanny said.

"Jeanny, if I'd wanted to erase a portion of the tape I wouldn't have left such obvious tracks."

"That's why I'm here. That's why I haven't turned the case over to the action section."

"That I appreciate," Pat said. "Look, honey, I need a little time. I know this old bird here. I know him like a friend, inside out. I need to have a long, long talk with him."

"I just can't allow you to be alone on board," Jeanny said, "and I have work to do back at the office."

"Come on, Jeanny."

She shook her head. "Pat, dammit, if you get me into trouble—"

"You know better than that."

"All right, look. I can hold up notifying action section until tomorrow afternoon at the latest. I don't think you're going to find anything more than our techs found, but I'm willing to give you the chance. On one condition. I want to know what the hell you were up to out there and who it is you suspect might have tampered with your computer."

"Later," he said. He didn't think he could talk about Corinne without displaying emotion. Jeanny knew him too well. He didn't want to have to admit to her that he had been suckered in by a bunch of city slickers from Zede II and made to look like a complete fool by a redheaded film star.

"Now," Jeanny said.

"I had a passenger. That was my main gig going to Taratwo, to pick up a woman—"

"Ah," Jeanny said.

"—and take her back to Zede II. What they didn't

tell me was that the Man, Brenden, didn't want the woman to leave his comfortable bed." And even as he said it a fist closed over his heart. But after what she'd done, what else could he believe? One lie almost guaranteed others. And she'd not only stolen Murphy's Stone, she'd fooled around with the computer while he was ill.

"Do you think she erased the tape?"

"That's not the only possibility," Pat said. "There's this. The ship went nowhere except the places which are recorded on tape. Once the computer located our position, I blinked onto the route and then we went straight down the route to Zede II. The computer had been cranky. Maybe that glitch there, which indicates that the delete button was pushed after going through half a dozen fail-safe's is a computer glitch. If so, maybe I can reproduce it."

"What are the other possibilities?" Jeanny asked.

"I was off the ship for a night on Zede II," he said. "Zede City Port is a big one, with all the modern equipment. Someone might have used some pretty sophisticated gear to bypass my security system, get on board, get into the computer."

"Why?"

"Why? I don't know. It's just a possibility."

"I still think the best bet is the passenger," Jeanny said.

"I don't think she had enough computer training to be able to do it," Pat said. "She'd have had to do it by oral order, and the old man was, and is, cranky, fancying himself to be hard of hearing."

"So you think you'd have heard her talking, even if you were asleep at the time?"

"Yeah," Pat said. Now why didn't he just tell Jeanny that he'd come down with the mindheat fever? He'd been out for days. Corinne had had plenty of time to carry on lengthy conversations with the old man.

"OK, Audrey," she said, and he didn't even bother to tell her not to call him Audrey. "You have about twenty-four hours."

He had the servo make coffee, pulled himself up to the computer console, settled in. First he told the old man to run a comprehensive check of all functions during the time period beginning with the first blink after the ship was lost in space. There was a mass of material, because the computer monitored all functions of all the ship's systems. He couldn't afford to skip over any of it, not even the inventory of stores in the nutrition servos. An unskilled computer operator might just have had to hunt and seek for a successful way to get the old man to erase, or at least push the delete button on the trip log.

Nothing is ever wasted, he felt, after he'd spent four hours checking the boring, seemingly endless catalog of ship's functions, because that minute examination told him just how well *Skimmer* functioned. He was proud of her. As for the computer, those automatic functions were carried out as smoothly as if the machine had been fresh off the assembly line.

The fact was that the ship could not have gone anywhere not recorded on the tape because he'd been lost in delirium and fever for seven and a half days. When he tabulated the time he was shocked. As he remembered it—and he couldn't be sure of his memory, when he'd asked Corinne how long he'd been out he was still pretty weak—she'd told him that he'd been ill five days.

That was when he first began to think that maybe the ship had been moved and that maybe the tape had been erased. She'd said five days. The computer showed a seven-and-a-half-day period of nutrition-servo operation between the first blink onto the route and the next leap down the route toward Zede II.

"All right, old man, let's check that," he said, typing orders rapidly. He was looking at the engine-room log now, beginning with the first blink after being lost. Nothing to it. Smooth as silk, the record of charges and discharges in the generator appeared. But just for kicks he decided to compare time—that missing seven and a half days—between the nutrition servo record and the engine-room record. He opposed the two sets of information.

It came out wrong.

It came out very, very wrong.

The measure of elapsed time on the engine-room record between the first blink onto the route and the next was exactly zero. In short, the record showed that the two blinks had been made with no elapsed time between. On the engine-room tape someone had done a very skillful job of alteration, taking out seven and a half days of routine monitorings by the computer.

Or were they seven and a half days of routine?

"Old man," he said, "you're not going to like this, but it's necessary." He flipped to oral mode. "Someone has been messing around in your innards," he said to the computer. "It would be nice if you could just tell me who."

"I'm sorry, you'll have to speak more distinctly," the computer said.

"Now, look, buddy," Pat said, "I know you're tired. You've got ionized contamination in your memory chambers, and you have to work harder to get a job done in some areas, but this is vital. If

I don't find out what happened out there they're
going to take the ship and you'll probably be carved
up for scrap."

A computer had no emotion. He had not asked
for a response and there was none. He was talking
to himself as much as to the old man.

"Do you have any record of someone other than
the captain using your facilities?" he asked. It was
a stab in the dark. The computer was not programmed to make such a distinction.

"There are no such records," the old man said.

He'd been hoping, since the old man was getting
cranky and independent, that he'd taken it on himself to make a note of the tampering.

"Is there recorded, anywhere in your memory,
any information regarding an order to delete material from any portion of your memory?"

"Wait one," the computer said, and went to work.

Pat settled back. The Century Series was not the
fastest computer ever built, but it was among the
most thorough, and had a storage capacity measured in the billions. Even at subatomic speed it
would take a while.

"There are no records of an order to delete material," the computer said, two cups of coffee later.

Outside, night came. Inside Pat had shed his
jacket, had eaten a sandwich, had enjoyed one
after-dinner drink, had made a dozen trips to the
sanitary closet to complete the flow of a half-dozen
cups of coffee through his system. He had the computer manual on his lap, and he was giving the old
man a real workout, coming at him from all angles, rephrasing questions, cross-checking by giving the computer opposing orders, going back again
and again to that time lapse between the first two
blinks toward Zede II.

It was a long night. The *Skimmer* was a living thing around him. The hatch was open so that the security guard could look in on him now and then, obviously at Jeanny's orders, so the heaters came on and hummed smoothly. There were clicks and hums, and once each hour the tiny ting of the chronometer and the chuckling and hissings of the old man as Pat exercised every part of his capacity, always coming back to the central question.

The chronometer tingled, and Pat glanced up. Three in the morning. He'd been at it since early afternoon. He felt as if he'd been run over by a herd of Tigian buffalo. His mouth was stale and brown from coffee, his head fuzzy, aching.

He went at the old man once again, head on, his voice a bit hoarse from talking. "The delete button was used," he said. "It was used on the trip log and on the engine-room log. Material was erased. I want to know how much material, old man. I want to know who did it. I want to know how she bypassed the fail-safes." For now he had accepted the fact that only Corinne could have done it, and that she'd done it during those seven and a half days while he was delirious with fever.

"There are no records of such actions," the old man said, not at all perturbed. He could go on with the game forever. He didn't get tired.

Pat took a break, walked to the hatch, and looked outside. The guard had been changed. The new man was young, and he looked miserable standing there in the chill of early morning.

"Why don't you come into the lock?" Pat asked. "We can button up and put some heat into it."

"Orders," the guard said. "But I appreciate the thought."

Pat went back inside, looked at the old man,

winking and blinking peacefully, hated him for a moment or two, drew one more cup of coffee. A thought came to him, something he hadn't checked. "Information on a fever known as mindheat fever, reference Taratwo."

The long session had accomplished one thing, however minor. The computer was no longer pretending to be hard of hearing.

"No information," the old man droned.

"Double-check."

"No information."

"Diseases indigenous to the planet Taratwo," he ordered.

"The planet Taratwo is unique among known planets in that the evolution of viral and bacterial forms is still in a primitive stage. Ash and smoke are health hazards on the planet, and there have been recorded cases of disease carried to the planet from other areas of habitation. On the Standard Star Index of Public Health, Taratwo is listed as the fourth most disease-free planet."

"General reference, health and disease. Check for mindheat fever."

That took a while. Finally, "There is no reference to mindheat fever. The two words, mind and heat, are not referenced as a unit. However, on the standard list of pharmaceuticals there is a synthetic drug, dexiapherzede, developed on Wagner's Planet, Zede system, which in the illegal drug trade is called heat."

"Depth search," Pat said, a feeling of revulsion in his stomach.

"Dexiapherzede was developed for use in treatment of depression. In regulated doses the effect on the patient is a feeling of well-being. In overdose the effect is hallucinatory. Moderate overdoses release the unconscious mind into dominance, and the hallucinations can be somewhat guided by the conscious mind into paths of pleasure or sensuous imagination. Heavier overdoses overwhelm the conscious mind and hallucinations are not controllable. Very heavy overdoses irritate the nerve tissue and are sometimes fatal, always accompanied by loss of consciousness and high fever."

Ah, Corinne.

"Time period of adverse effects of an extreme overdose?"

"Dexiapherzede is fragile, quickly assimilated and rapidly metabolized by the human body. A nonfatal overdose produces hallucinations and fever for approximately twelve hours, depending on the individual rate of metabolism."

Seven and a half days. She'd have had to dose him with that junk over a dozen times.

One more question. "Does dexiapherzede leave any detectable residue in the human body?"

"Heavy overdose amounts of the drug do moderate damage to certain cells in the liver. The effects of this damage are self-reparable by the liver over a period of some weeks."

So if she had drugged him it could be proved by a check of his liver. He paced the bridge. He could remember her face as if it were before him in one of her pictures, and in that face he simply could not find the cruelty which would be necessary to put a man through the agony he'd experienced. He could still remember some of those nightmares. They'd been coming at him at night ever since his illness, and they were no child's nightmares. They were full-grown and damned mean nightmares that made him wake up in a cold sweat.

So, she'd drugged him. Why? Just to sit on the ship for seven and a half days and play games with the computer? No. It was becoming more and more evident that Corinne Tower had been a much better actress than he'd suspected. She'd pretended ignorance of ship's operations, but she'd taken the *Skimmer* somewhere while he was under the influence of the drug, somewhere she didn't want him to know about. And she'd been good enough at computers to get past several guards in the trip log, and to erase the engine-room monitoring tape so smoothly that it wasn't noticeable unless compared for time lapse with another tape. Sharp, but not sharp enough to erase the time lapse on the other monitoring tapes, such as the nutrition servos. Sharp, but not sharp enough to see that she'd left just a tiny little glitch on the trip log, just enough to catch the attention of Central's computer.

"She drugged me, old man. She put me under for over a week. What did she do for a week?"

He dived back into his work. For a week she'd eaten—that was shown by the nutrition-servo tapes. She'd used the toilet; this was shown by the sanitary-system tapes. She'd even watched a couple of movies. Calm as calm. Sitting there watching pictures while he fought monsters and sweated blood.

But, as dawn came, and the guard changed outside, he was no closer to the answer. "Dammit," he said, "what else did she do? Did she move the ship?"

"There is no record on the trip log of the ship's having been moved," the computer said.

"Did she charge the generator?"

"There is no record on the engine-room log of the generator's being charged."

Pat was grasping at straws. "Print out the last two responses."

There is no record on the trip log of the ship's having been moved. There is no record on the engine-room log of the generators being charged.

"All right, old man," Pat said. "I'm beginning to get the idea that you know something I don't know. What do you know that I don't?"

"I am programmed in many fields of knowledge," the computer said. "Perhaps I know little that you do not, in a sense, know, having been exposed to the information at one period or another of your existence. However, my capacity to recall such information is, by the nature of computers and human brains, greater."

"A philosopher, yet," Pat said. But still there was something. It tickled at his brain, made him feel that he was near a breakthrough.

"I still say," he muttered, "that you know something I don't know. What is it, dammit?"

"The question is very general," the computer said. "It will require that you transcribe all that you know. At that time I will compare your knowledge with that recorded in my chambers and give you your answer."

"Go to hell," Pat said, rising, thinking that if he drank one more cup of coffee he'd turn brown, drawing it anyhow. He looked down at the last printed lines.

There is no record. There is no record.

He consulted the computer manual. Somewhere in those small but almost infinitely capacious memory chambers, even with the ionization, there had to be something that would tell him what Corinne had done with those seven and a half days. He thumbed through the thick book. It would take days, weeks, for him to check every function, every area of storage. He didn't have the time. Jeanny would drag him off the *Skimmer* kicking and screaming in about seven hours.

The Century Series of computer was a sophisticated piece of technology. In a way, a Century which was ship-mounted corresponded in function with the human brain. A part of the Century operated on what could be compared to the conscious level of the human mind. Another part was much like the unconscious part of the human mind which kept house, operated the multitude of involuntary functions of the system, told the eyes to blink so many times a second without the conscious mind having to remember, kept the heart beating, enzymes and mysterious little fluids flowing, the nerves doing their thing. The old man performed such a function aboard ship, monitoring and controlling the *Skimmer*'s systems. The computer itself controlled the mundane but vital functions of that second-to-second, day-to-day ship's housekeeping. On the "conscious" level, the computer responded to its human controller.

Pat began to read about the computer's automatic functions, got interested, but got nowhere closer to the solution of the problem. He was about to put the manual aside and go back to his oral quizzing of the computer when he saw the heading "Space Law." Since he was in violation of the law, he decided to read it. Found the section regarding the penalties for tampering with the trip log, got a chill when it was confirmed that X&A could lift his license and seize the *Skimmer*. Gloom piled atop doom.

"What do you know about space law?" he asked the old man.

"All relevant information is contained . . ." And the computer gave reference numbers for a particular memory chamber.

"Let's take a look," Pat said.

The computer began to recite space law.

"Skip to the section regarding the trip log," Pat ordered.

"Access to the trip log is limited to manufacturer and X&A," the computer said.

"Just tell me about it," Pat said.

The computer gave reference numbers.

"What would it take for an unauthorized person to get access to that section?"

"The exact access code."

"How does one get the exact access code?"

"The access code is known only to the manufacturer and X&A."

"Ah," Pat said. "Where were you manufactured, old man?"

"I am a product of Century Subatomics, Inc."

"And where is Century Subatomics located?"

"The three facilities of Century Subatomics, Inc., are located on the planet Zede II. Plant number one is twenty-two point three three miles south-southeast of Zede City—"

"OK," Pat said. He felt as if he was getting close to something. "If an unauthorized person had the exact access code to the trip log memory chamber and used it, would you keep a record?"

"Yes."

"OK, let's see that record."

"The record is kept in—" The computer gave the

numbers for the trip log chamber with a sub-
number. "Access only to X&A's central computer."

Great. But not bad. He could call Jeanny and get
her to connect with the old man from down at
X&A and see who had used the access code last.

Jeanny was still in bed. "God," she moaned,
"have you been up all night?"

"Jeanny, get down to the office as quick as you
can. Plug into my computer and check in the trip
log section and I think you're going to find out
that I wasn't the one who ordered the erasure."

"Tell you what," she said. "I'll call you back
after breakfast when I get to work."

"Jeanny—"

"Oh, hell. I'll call the duty man. He'll check and
give you a call."

He drank another cup of coffee and went to the
sanitary closet twice, and then the duty man was
on the communicator.

"Captain Howe, this is highly irregular. However, I have checked, as Captain Thompson re-
quested, and the last access to your trip log was by
an authorized computer at X&A."

"And before that?"

"The authorized computer at Xanthos Central."

"And before that?"

"I must warn you, Captain, that I have recorded
the following information for the action section of
X&A. Prior to the last two authorized accesses by
X&A and Xanthos Central a deletion has been made.
It is serious enough to erase the record of blinks
from the trip log, Captain. This is the first inci-
dence I've encountered where the computer's record of access has been altered. Someday, when
you get out of jail, I'd like you to tell me how you

managed to break the fail-safes and get the access code."

"You've made my day," Pat said, closing off.

He slouched in the chair, beaten. The old man, calm as calm, blinked green lights at him in readiness, as if he wasn't tired of the game. "You heartless monster," Pat said.

"You are drawing a comparison which has no relevance," the old man said.

"You know, dammit. You're playing with me. You know and you won't tell me."

"I have been computing something you said previously," the old man said. "You asked me specifically what I know that you don't know. Is that correct?"

"That is correct. Do you have a different answer?"

"By a narrow definition of that question, relating it to your search for the missing segments on certain of my storage areas, I can say that I, apparently, know of one memory chamber."

"Access numbers," Pat ordered, feeling a surge of hope.

"There are no access numbers. This chamber is concerned with internal function of a Century Series computer."

"Depth search," Pat said.

"A capacity for self-diagnosis is built into the Century Series. This chamber is accessible to authorized repair technicians manually."

"What is the purpose of this chamber?" Pat asked.

"Between cleanings and repairs I note all abnormalities. Upon printout, the technician has a complete record of those abnormalities."

"Printout," Pat ordered.

"Printout of the self-diagnosis chamber is activated . . ." The computer went into a complicated technical explanation.

"Repeat that slowly, one instruction at a time," Pat ordered, after running to get his tool kit out of the mate's cabin.

He had removed an access plate, two plug-in circuit boards, and saw, just where the old man said it would be, a two-stage switch. He activated it. The computer began to spew out symbols in computer language and figures.

"What is all this?" Pat asked in exasperation.

"I am printing the development of ionization in chamber 73-R-45-B."

"Skip to sections relevant to alteration of the trip log," Pat ordered.

"I do not control this printout once it is underway."

"Great," Pat said.

He watched the paper emerge. It was covered with data of meaning only to the computer and a good computer tech.

It was difficult to be optimistic, with his time running out, but at least the new owner would have the self-diagnosis printout in case he wanted to keep *Skimmer* in service instead of junking her.

Coffee. Blah. The old man announcing the numbers of each chamber as he printed his own diagnosis. Pat sat up with a jerk as he recognized the number of the engine-room log. There were only a few abnormalities, and they were readable.

The following discharges and charges of the blink generator were erased on oral orders from an unidentified operator:

She'd gone a long way. She'd blinked the gener-

ator several times on the way out and several
times on the way back.

It was another thirty minutes, during which Pat
went quietly hyper, nerves jangling from too much
coffee, before the old man got to the section in his
self-diagnosis chamber which dealt with abnormalities in the chamber containing the trip log.

On oral orders from an unidentified operator
the following blink coordinates were deleted
from the trip log.

Pat whooped with joy. His hands were shaking
from coffee nerves. He had on the printout all the
coordinates for the blinks Corinne had taken while
he was out. He could check against charts and tell
where she'd taken the *Skimmer*. He was out of the
woods. All he had to do was call Jeanny and tell
her.

Tell her what?

He could imagine a stern-faced X&A hangman
saying, "The fact that, without your knowledge,
the computer kept a record of the blinks which
you erased does not lesson your guilt."

Damn. "Is that all, old man?"

Suddenly the printout was supplemented by
sound. First the old man's voice. "Space law states
that access to the trip log shall be by manufacturer and X&A only for the matter of alterations,
and for extracting information access is granted to
Xanthos Central Control or one of its substations.
Therefore, since an unidentified operator, not mentioned in space law, has ordered alterations of the
trip log, I have recorded for later identification
that operator's voice."

Pat whooped again, and then fell silent as Corinne's throaty, calm voice began to read off an

order to erase the following blinks, and then the numbers, still in that cool, throaty voice.

He caught Jeanny just as she was entering her office. "Get over here as quick as you can," he said. "And bring someone in authority with you."

"I'm the authority, Pat, until I turn it over to the action section."

"Then get over here, Jeanny, please."

He was waiting for her with a hot cup of coffee just the way she liked it, with plenty of low-cal sweetener. He told her about the drug and then he showed her the self-diagnosis printout, let her hear Corinne's voice giving the illegal orders.

"Looks as if we can throw you in jail for being gullible, Audrey," she said.

He started to say it, but didn't, letting it pass. He'd had time to check the coordinates Corinne had used. They went right off any known chart into a region of crowded stars toward the galactic core. You didn't go too close to the core. The stars were dense there, and the chaos of interconnected magnetic and gravitational fields made navigation, and even survival, a nightmare. The massed stars put out storms of hot radiation which could cook anything living within the hull of a ship in seconds. But Corinne had gone toward that chaos, directly toward the heart of the galaxy, where that huge, fiery engine at the core gave off incredible energies.

Pat didn't tell Jeanny that he'd already checked the coordinates. Nor did he, for some reason, tell her about Murphy's Stone.

"I'd say that if we can find residue of that drug in your system, Pat, you have a good case for being reinstated," Jeanny said.

He was burning inside. His entire body was vibrating, coffee nerves, a caffeine rush. And more. He was burning to find out where she'd taken the ship, what was out there toward the core stars.

"What are you waiting for?" Jeanny asked. "Let's get over to the clinic."

Pat lay on a cold metal table, separated from the cold metal by a thin sheet. A monster of a machine lowered, buzzed. The results were in within minutes. There was superficial damage to liver cells. The damage was healing nicely. The damage was consistent with several known causes, among them an overdose of at least three separate drugs. Meanwhile, the analysis of his body fluids had been completed. A technician came into the room where Pat, dressed again, sat drinking coffee with Jeanny.

"Captain," the technician said, "I'd advise you to cut down on your intake of coffee. Your urine is discolored and I've never seen a higher caffeine level."

"Yeah, thanks," Pat said, putting down his cup.

"You do drugs often?" the technician asked.

"I do drugs never," Pat said.

The technician glanced at Jeanny with a knowing smile. "Sometime during the past few weeks you've taken a rather massive overdose of a little goodie which the druggies call heat, technical name dexiapherzede. I thought we'd just about done away with that one. We'd be interested in knowing, Captain, just where you got your hands on it."

"I'd like that report in writing in my office within the next hour," Jeanny said, rising.

Pat was merely a ship's captain. Jeanny Thompson was a captain in X&A. When she gave an order to a technician, that order was obeyed.

In her office, the report in hand, she looked at Pat with her eyes squinted. "All right, Audrey—"

"Don't call me Audrey," he said.

"—you're cleared. I've filed your reinstatement on the computer. If you leave Xanthos by ship within the next twenty-four hours you might have to have Central check with me. It takes a while to counter-act something as serious as having your license lifted."

"Jeanny, when I get back, the best dinner for you, and a nice little gift."

"So you are going?"

"Wouldn't you?"

"I don't know. I might just write off my losses and forget it. You were playing in the big time on that trip to Taratwo, Pat. Maybe out of your class. You're alive, and our scan on your affairs showed that you made a bundle out of the trip. Why don't you just stay here, get the overhaul completed on *Skimmer*?"

To that point she'd been all business. Now her facial expression softened. "I have two weeks of vacation coming up. If you'd like some company when you take the ship out for a check ride after the overhaul—"

"Jeanny, that sounds great," he said. "Hold that vacation until I get back, OK?"

She shrugged. "Have yourself a ball," she said, standing, making it clear that she was dismissing him.

FIVE

Skimmer lifted into space with her hull still showing the dullness of the thousand-parsec syndrome.
Pat had taken time only to restock the food sup-
plies and pick out a few new movies. The first part
of the trip was routine, along well-maintained blink
routes, and he was able to program several blinks
at one time, then let the old man do the work. The
long oral sessions with the computer seemed to
have had an invigorating effect. There was, at first,
no indication of the sluggishness associated with
ionization of the memory chambers.

Pat didn't have a cup of coffee for three days. He
used the time to try to make estimates, a difficult
task, of just how far toward the core of the galaxy
Corinne's route would take him.

He passed within a few light-years of Zede II,
then began to retrace the route *Skimmer* had followed in taking Corinne home. It was difficult not
to think of her. X&A had made some preliminary
inquiries, based on the solid evidence in the old
man's self-diagnosis chamber, and had run head-on
into a gaggle of space lawyers who said that Corinne Tower, the famous Zedeian holo star, had

not been off Zede II in over five years, and that any half-baked space mercenary who said that she had was risking a libel suit.

Well, it was X&A's baby now. Since there was no record of Corinne Tower holding a space license there was little X&A could do, even if its investigators did wade through the banks of lawyers. Pat guessed that they'd file the information and forget it. That was all right with him. He couldn't bring himself to want to see Corinne punished. Not while he was there alone on the ship, remembering how she looked when she first awoke in the morning and came out of the mate's cabin for breakfast.

As the days passed and the nightmares began to fade, he began to rationalize her actions. All right, so she was a professional actress. So her tenderness, that one time that he'd kissed her, could have been sheer acting. Certainly she'd doublecrossed him. She'd stolen his diamond, or at least his half of the diamond. It was sort of pleasant to think of what he could have done with half of the value of Murphy's Stone, but what would he do with himself if he were fabulously wealthy? He didn't take on sometimes dangerous assignments just for the thrill of it. He did it for money, but did he really want the things that megamillions could buy?

Hell, yes. The newest and best in space yachts, manor houses on the most pleasant planets, some of those beautiful and awesome light-brush paintings by Anleian of Selbelle III which brought millions at auction. Hell, yes. But what the hell. What he wanted most was what he couldn't even hope to have. He could hope for another big strike. He'd made one, in Murphy's Stone, so he could make another and have the yacht and the houses and the paintings. What he couldn't have was Corinne, and it was, he realized, that loss which was sending him out and away from UP space into uncharted space. If he couldn't have her he had to know why. He couldn't believe, down in his heart, that she could have acted that scene when he kissed her, when the quiet tears came as she fought against the desires of her own body.

The first part of the trip, reversing the course they'd traveled together, was preliminary. The big show got underway after he'd reached the first blink beacon they'd found after those lovely days of being lost and alone in space. He punched in the coordinates of the first jump Corinne had taken alone and held his breath. Three jumps later the old man was going bananas, because Pat wouldn't give him time to make those time-consuming 360-degree scans for points of identification.

The star patterns were entirely different. The massive glow of the Milky Way was before them, growing dense. The blinks were becoming shorter because of increasing star population, and all the stars were alone, bright solitaires in space, without a comforting family of planets. That's the way it was in toward the core, and that was the main reason why all of X&A's exploration efforts were directed toward less densely starred areas out toward the periphery.

The only suns with planets which were known to be tucked away amid that glaring, hard chaos of stars toward the core were nowhere near Pat's route, but off at a bearing of about 45 degrees to his port. He'd been there. Once after he'd finished a particularly profitable trip he'd taken a sweet young girl from Xanthos University, a former student, not that much younger than himself, to cruise slowly by a dozen worlds which had, at some time in the distant past, been sterilized by some unimaginable weapon. The Dead Worlds. Hundreds of expeditions had searched for their secret. The rubble piled over bedrock showed, in minutes bits and pieces, that once a thriving civilization had existed there on each of the closely packed planets of an odd grouping of a family of interrelated stars. And because of that rubble, because of that total destruction of a dozen worlds, X&A ships went armed with weapons of war which had not been used in a thousand years. For any race which could pulverize a dozen civilizations had to have potent weapons, and on each X&A expedition there were two hopes among the crew. One, that they'd find a sweet, beautiful water planet with livable conditions and, possibly, an intelligent race with whom man could exchange ideas and information, no longer alone in a big, big universe. Two, that they would not encounter the beings who had reduced the Dead Worlds to rubble lying loosely atop bedrock.

Space, to a man alone, engenders a variety of thoughts. Pat thought of the Dead Worlds, and wondered if he'd find anything like that up ahead, where the stars were densely packed and a confusion of solar winds from that vast population of suns sent radiation counters clattering. He thought mostly of Corinne, just a little about a two-week vacation with Jeanny, and scolded himself because he couldn't work up much enthusiasm for the latter. And he remembered his drug-induced nightmares, tried to sort them, identify them as spinoffs of childhood horrors, things he'd heard, things he'd read. After all, the unconscious can't create. It merely stores, like a computer, and distorts stored information in seemingly random patterns.

It was interesting to analyze his nightmares. He could identify three or four childhood dreams, dreams which were fairly common. He had flown in his illness, soaring, pumping his legs against air to gain altitude—that, of course, a distortion by the unconscious of the act of swimming upward toward the surface of a pool after diving deep. He had fled unseen terror fighting against clinging, molasses-like resistance. He couldn't trace that one back to any known influence. He had gnashed his teeth in his fever, feeling them crumble and fall out in pieces. That, of course, went back to childhood and the first traumatic loss of baby teeth, or, perhaps, to adult visits to the dentist.

Monsters he could remember from his nightmares during that time were really not so monstrous. Upon analysis, they became nothing more than composites from horror movies, legends, stories.

There was one thing, however, that he could not trace back. His memory of the entire episode was hazy, dredged up with difficulty and little clarity, but twice during the trip outward from Xanthos he had seen in his dream a huge, centuries-old starship, hull marked and battered, floating alone in space, dead, silent. He supposed that his unconscious mind had composed the ship from space-opera stories or movies, but still that memory seemed to have a solidity that the others from the fevered period lacked.

Skimmer's generator had no difficulty charging when he had emptied it with the multiple blinks which led him even closer to the core, ever deeper, by zig and zag past blue giants and white dwarfs, all the various types of stars, some of them very, very old, some of them surprisingly young.

There was a school of astrophysics which theorized that stars were continually being created there in the inaccessible heart, in the core heat of the galaxy. Pat chose not to believe that. He believed in a single act of creation and, although he was not pious or devout, in a single creator. When Pat's God said, "Let there be light," there was *light*, the Big Bang, a light never seen before or since. Faced with an act of creation, he had to accept a creator, and that rather pleased him. He couldn't accept the orthodox opinion that God spent his time watching sparrows fall and listening to every prayer by the pious. He imagined God to be a bit too busy for that, but there, nevertheless.

Deep and shallow thoughts while alone. The old man chuckling and complaining because the ship was hopelessly lost, except for Corinne's series of blink coordinates, the ship functioning perfectly, Pat back on coffee. No blink beacons. And yet it was impossible for a ship to have established the route by random blinks. One random blink there near the core and the ship would never emerge, having merged forever with the molten subatomic particles of the sun. No. Someone, in some ship, at some time, had had to feel his way along that route, perhaps at sublight speeds, although that was farfetched, because a ship traveling at sublight speeds would have taken not just one generation but several to chart that route and leave blink coordinates. More likely the course was charted as X&A ships now charted new blink routes, making blinks to the safe extent of their optical and sensor scouting ability, covering short, short distances in an instant, then taking hours to determine how far the next blink can take them without contact with a solid body.

Even with the X&A method it would have taken years, decades, to chart the route. *Skimmer*'s track on the chart being constructed by the computer extended backward far and away in that zigzagging line out toward the areas where the stars were thinner.

It was hard work. Corinne had made the trip there and back in seven and a half days. At the end of three days, with only a few catnaps while the depleted generator drew on the energies of the stars themselves for its charge, he had just one more blink to make to be at the end of Corinne's course. He forced himself to wait for a full generator charge. He wanted to have all the power he could when he blinked out at the end of his journey. He had no idea what he'd find there and if it had teeth, he'd have to rely on that brute of a generator in *Skimmer*'s engine room to make more multiple blinks than whatever it was that had teeth. He had two hours' sleep, awoke, ate. Corinne looked almost frail, but she'd been tough enough to go without sleep in more than two-hour segments for at least six days and look fresh and beautiful when he came out of his drugged condition.

"OK, old man," he said, when the generator was charged to a capacity which so energized the whole of *Skimmer* that the hairs on his arms and hands tingled. "Here we go."

Tensed, he waited for the alarms to start whining, clanging, shouting. A calm computer told him that he was one quarter of an astronomical unit from a planet about the size of ancient Mars in the Solar System, and that the planet emanated no energies other than the natural reflections of the solar winds of a weak yellow star which was only a small disk in the distance.

He gave it some time. He scanned the planet. It was a planet of rock and sand, barren, and yet it showed an atmosphere. Men had settled worse planets, drawing the subterranean water upward to the surface, altering the climate with imported plant life.

Nothing happened. All sensors working showed no danger, no manmade emanations. He put *Skimmer* on flux and made his approach. When he could distinguish surface features on the planet he saw barren mountain ranges, deep chasms. Once the planet had lived, had built mountains, had shot hot lava and rock into the air, had possessed surface water to cut those massive gorges.

The planet hung over him now, the *Skimmer* in orbit, all sensors and instruments at work. The only change in readings was a hint of water in a narrow belt around the equator. That was only mildly interesting. The optics picked up hints of green in that belt. More interesting. And it became even more interesting when a half-dozen alarms clanged and whistled and whined at the same time and the old man broke his sulky silence.

"Alert, alert. Unidentified vessel."

She came swimming toward the *Skimmer* in a slightly higher orbit, clearing the curve of the planet with stately, slow, majestic movement, a huge ship.

Pat jerked on the arms-control helmet, went into action. The alarms were quieted. The computer spat out information. There was no radiation of any kind coming from the huge ship. There were no overt signs of hostile intent.

The ship looked very familiar to Pat. It took him only seconds to realize that the ship which moved slowly and majestically toward him in an orbit which would bring it almost directly over the *Skimmer* was the ship of his nightmares.

He threw the optics on highest magnification. The ship expanded on his screen. The hull showed multiples of the effects of the thousand-parsec syndrome. Pat waited. She was almost spherical in shape, a design from the past, and she had a feeling, a sense of age. She was close enough now so that he could see the closed ports which, in all probability, housed weapons. There was no sign of life, no emanations detectable by the *Skimmer*'s array of instruments.

When she was directly overhead he could see the exit ports. They were open. The ship was dead in space, open to space, silent, deserted, eerie.

When she had disappeared behind the curve of the planet, her discolored hull sending back one gleaming flash of reflected sunlight from the weak yellow sun, he went to the computer and punched up a tape on spaceship design and history.

The ship which was in a high, stable orbit around this barren planet in an area where there should not even be a planet, so near the core that the huge, fiery monsters, the crowded stars, seemed to push down, to overwhelm, was of a type which had not been built for a thousand years. She was an ancient colonization ship, a ship of the type used in the days of early expansion outward from the core of the UP, a ship whose only purpose was to carry masses of people, with their possessions, to a new home among the stars.

SIX

There are few things in existence which attain infinite perfection. The universe itself is flawed, for it is not eternal. All of it, all that small portion known to man and that vast unknown portion, is on a minutely slow slide to nothing, expending energies which cannot, short of another creation, be replaced. Someday it will all be cold, and motionless, and sterile. An orchid approaches perfection, but nevertheless is subject to mutation, environmental damage, and swift decay.

Of all the things that approach perfection, Pat Howe thought, as he exited *Skimmer*'s airlock, space comes closest in quality to the absolute perfection of loneliness. No man is ever more alone than a man in self-contained space gear outside the frail protection of the hull of his ship.

He had dosed himself heavily with radiation preventatives, and had the after-exposure doses ready on the bridge to take when he returned. *Skimmer* was on her own, in the care of the old man. He left her with the out hatch open, the inner hatch of the airlock closed. He pushed off, and the movement gave him a slow tumbling motion which he counteracted with the control jets. Then he was one man alone, a tiny mote in the glare of those claustrophobic star fields, one side of his suit being cooled by frantically working units, the other side being warmed until he was out of *Skimmer*'s shadow and the full impact of the solar winds from the thousands of stars hit him, sending the counter clattering.

Skimmer was parked in a matching orbit less than a hundred yards from the ancient, giant colonization ship. Pat looked back, just once. The ship looked dearly familiar, warm, inviting. There was a great urge in him to go back, run for the airlock, close the hatch behind him, and seek safety within *Skimmer*'s friendly confines.

But somehow, the woman he loved, or had loved, had obtained the access codes to the computer's restricted chambers. The Zede connection had to be the answer—the "businessmen." He guessed that if an investigation could plow through to the heart of the matter there'd be a traceable link between Corinne's "film producers" and Century Subatomics. Simple enough for the right people to get the access codes from company records. Which meant, of course, that they had had to have the serial number of the computer on *Skimmer*. Had they come up with the computer number and the access codes and then come to seek him out, or had they found him, then obtained the access codes?

None of that really mattered, except as a question of curiosity. What mattered was Corinne's motivation.

Jetting carefully toward the big ship, he had time to wonder just what significance the ship had. Obviously, it had been the destination of Corinne's solo trip. What had been on the ship which was important enough to make her drug him and take a long, tiresome trip into the area near the galactic core? If she had taken something from that ancient derelict it had been small, for she'd left the ship with only her one bag, and a good bit of the storage area inside the bag had been taken up by Murphy's Stone.

He eased himself up to the hull of the old ship near a large, gaping hatch, pulled himself along to the hatch using magnetic clingers, moved his head to shine his helmet light into the dark interior. The inner hatch of the lock was also open. That part of the big ship, at least, was open to space, cold, dead. According to the information he had from *Skimmer*'s library, such ships had carried four to six space launches. There were tiedowns for such a launch in the lock which he entered, using the suit's jets to swim clear of the discolored bulkheads and decking.

The airlock was empty, any speck or mote of loose dust sucked into the insatiable maw of space's vacuum long ago.

Fighting an urge to keep looking over his shoulder, he floated into a corridor, his way lit only by the helmet light. The corridor was as bare as the lock. Brackets on the bulkheads showed that some kind of equipment, perhaps spacesuits or safety gear, had been removed.

He contacted the computer on *Skimmer*. "Give me the shortest route to the control areas," he said.

The computer, checking Pat's oral reports against the plans for similar ships from *Skimmer*'s information store, sent Pat on a route which took him toward the core of the ship, heading for a point on the opposite side where the control bridge perched on the outside circumference of the huge sphere.

Since he was near, he detoured into the engine areas.

It became quickly obvious to him that the ship had not met with some totally damaging disaster, but had been abandoned, and not in panic. The ship had been thoroughly cannibalized. All movable equipment and gear had been removed, and the gold shielding of the almost unbelievably huge and antique blink drive had been removed. It had been necessary, in the technology of a thousand years past, to use a lot of gold for shielding. It was all gone, and the more accessible parts of the generator itself had been removed.

He passed through an area of living quarters to find the same conditions. In places, even the dividing bulkheads had been ripped out, presumably for reclamation of the lightweight metals therein.

Far down in the guts of the ship, alone in a silence which caused a continuous reaction in his inner ears, a vacuous, almost unrealized hissing which was the psychological reaction to the total absence of sound, he could hear his own heart beating, could sense the song of his blood as it was pumped through his veins.

He whirled once, swiftly, panic causing his heart to race, for there in the closeness of the engineering spaces his fully alerted senses had given him a false signal of movement where there was only vacuum, and space-discolored bulkheads and stripped-down machinery.

"Whoa, Pat," he said. "No ghosts here. They didn't die here. They left the ship."

Although he sent the words aloud to the old man, the computer made no reply. It was not programmed for small talk.

He found the instrument and computer sections

before he reached the bridge. Computers had been quite large when the ship was built. They were still using microchips then, but the microchips had all been removed. He'd been hoping to find a few in place. He could have rigged the old man to read them, if indeed, information had lasted for a thousand years. But even the light-metal access doors had been removed.

The viewports on the control bridge were open. Radiation had clouded the plastic of the ports, so that it now acted as an inefficient filter for the storm of particles which swirled constantly around the ship.

And on the bridge, as elsewhere, all instruments, anything movable, had been removed. There was not so much as a scrap of paper, a mote of dust, a small personal item left behind to give him a clue.

He found the reason for the ship's abandonment in the guidance and navigational section. There had been a severe explosion, and a resulting fire. That he could tell by twisted shards of metal and scorch marks, but the people of the ship had gutted that section, too.

"Old man," he said, "do you think it would be worthwhile to search the ship? I mean every compartment, every nook and cranny?"

"Such a course would give the most available information," the computer said.

Pat felt a little shiver. The damned ship was big. He'd have to make several trips back to *Skimmer* to recharge the suit's life-support gear. It would take days. And each time he stuck his head into a new hole, the beam of light from his helmet doing not the world's best job of dispelling the total darkness, he felt that shiver come again. He persisted, however, until he had located the ship's library. There'd been a fire there, too, for the library, although there was no direct connection, backed the section which had taken the full force of the explosion. The fire must have been fed by an oxygen-rich mixture, for in the library area, identifiable by the twisted, ruined, gutted pans which had once held computer tapes, even light metals had been consumed.

He was within thirty minutes of having to go on reserve on the suit's life-support system. There was one more thing he wanted to check. He found a small exit hatch open near the control areas and did the checking from space, jetting around the globe of the ancient ship to locate all six of the airlocks where once the space launches had been stored. All were empty. All the launches had been used.

For what? There was but one answer. For some reason the old colony ship had chosen to explore toward the core, and, following a slow and erratic course, dodging stars, had found a planet. It was not much of a planet. It loomed over Pat's head as he jetted back toward *Skimmer*, colorful, true, with red and orange pigments in the barren areas, but poor as planets go. So the ship had found the planet, *before* the explosion had destroyed its ability to maneuver, and the people had left the disabled ship on the space launches. The launches were not lifeboats. If there'd been a full complement of colonists aboard, enough to people those warrens of quarters, the launches would have had to make several trips. There was only one place which could have been a destination for such back-and-forth ferrying. The planet.

He'd set the computer to analyzing the planet during his absence. He checked over the information while he was taking the multiple doses of after-exposure drugs, washing them down with coffee. There was a viable atmosphere, surprisingly rich in oxygen. There was a bit of surface water, much of it frozen into thin icecaps at the poles, some of it in the greenbelt around the equator. The deep basins which once had been oceans were arid. The tall mountains were eroded only slightly in areas, showing that they'd been formed late in the planet's wet period, before something happened to stop the rains, and the water which had filled the vast ocean spaces had disappeared, evaporating into space, or sinking into porous rock.

There was enough carbon dioxide in the atmosphere to block out most of the harmful radiation from the suns which surrounded the small area of open space occupied by the planet and its small star.

In spite of the fact that *Skimmer*'s state-of-the-art sensors and instruments showed no evidence of life on the scrubby planet, Pat made his preparations for a low-level scouting run with care. *Skimmer* lowered through atmosphere on her flux thrusters, leveled off at ten thousand feet with all her eyes and ears on full amplification, her shield up, her skipper wearing the fire-control helmet, the computer humming and purring as it digested and correlated the flood of data.

It was pretty good down there. Good air. Water just under the surface, close enough so that several species of vegetation existed. The greenest areas were on low ground, at the lowest points of what had once been ocean beds.

It didn't occur to Pat until he had taken *Skimmer* halfway around the circumference of the planet at the equator, passing through the night zone into sunlight, that he might have himself a planet. He wouldn't own all of it. There were too few habitable planets to allow one man or a small group of men to claim an entire world by right of discovery, but there was a well-established reward system. To qualify for right of discovery he'd have to prove that the planet was unrecorded on X&A charts, and that it was uninhabited.

He didn't know, for a moment, whether to hope to find descendants of the survivors of the big colonization ship or to hope that there was no intelligent life down there. He didn't have too long to muse over it, however, because the computer was sending him a shrill little warning from one particular instrument which worked only when a ship was very close to a particular form of life which emanated the faint results of oxygen-based metabolism.

"Oh ho," Pat said. There were, after all, people, or at least animal forms, down there.

He saw the village on the optics screen just after the computer had alerted him. He put *Skimmer* on hover and let the ship's instruments and sensors work, but he could see himself that there were artifacts of man there, log cabins with thatched roofs, cultivated fields. He ordered the computer to try contact on all known wavelengths. He didn't really expect an answer, because there were no energy emanations, just the detection of combustion, wood smoke, coming from the chimneys of several of the cabins.

The village was connected, he saw, as he lifted *Skimmer* for an overall view of the area ahead, to other villages by a network of roads. The roads were not paved. There was no evidence of grading, for there was no need for it in that rainless climate. The roads showed an overall pattern which intrigued him. He moved *Skimmer* again and hovered over a large stone building, low, walls high, apparently thick, and sloping slightly upward toward a roof which was paved with light metals in slabs, slabs taken from the partitions which had been removed from the abandoned colony ship in orbit around the planet.

OK. So he wasn't going to get discovery rights to a planet. It was, obviously, populated, and by the descendants of the people who had come on the big ship.

From the stone building, the roads radiated out like the spokes of a wheel to the outlying villages. Obviously, the stone building was the center of things. The ship's sensors were picking up life emanations in quantity in the villages and in the central area, where the same style of rude cabins lined the streets radiating out from the stone building.

Pat decided not to land at the heart of that little community of villages, not because he was afraid for himself, but for the safety of the people down there. It was obvious that they'd reverted to primitivism and had shown little advancement in the thousand or so years they'd been on the planet. No telling what they remembered about the civilization which had sent them forth. They might see *Skimmer* as a threat and attack, and Pat didn't want to have to use modern weapons, even in self-defense, against people armed, perhaps, with bows and arrows.

He picked a rather isolated hut near the outskirts of one of the outlying villages. He lowered the ship on flux, saw, as the ground neared, that there were two men, yes, men, standard model, unmutated, two arms, two legs, one head, working in a field near the isolated cabin.

They heard the whispering thunder of *Skimmer*'s flux thrusters, dropped their tools, and stood, faces upturned, as the ship blew dust and lowered to squat about a hundred yards from them. They continued to stare as Pat opened the hatch.

Man knew little about his origins. History estimated that only a small number of people, perhaps less than one million, left Old Earth before nuclear war devastated the planet, riding outward from that small, isolated sun on ships far more primitive than the old colony ship which circled this world.

The people from Old Earth had settled, it was felt, only four or five planets in the original wave of colonization from Old Earth. Various portions of the UP claimed to have been the original points of settlement, including the older planets of the Zede system. In all cases, the small groups of settlers were unable to maintain, on virgin planets, the level of technology which had sent them into space. In fact, the best estimates of historians were that it had taken between ten and thirty thousand years for the space children of Old Earth to soar back out among the stars.

It was felt that one Old Earth "country," or, perhaps, a small group of "countries," had been responsible for sending the starships up, for there was a surprising singularity of racial types in the entire race of UP man. Earth history was nothing more than semimyth, or legend, but the old tales said that on Old Earth, there had been red men and yellow men, black men and brown men, and light-skinned men like modern man. And legend/myth said that each different type of man on Old

Earth had had his own language. Some historians said that that fact alone would have accounted for Earth's constant warfare which led to the final conflagration.

Only a specialist, such as ex-professor Pat Howe, understood the concept of different languages. There'd been a brief flurry of interest in the popular media when an expedition brought back from the colliding galaxies in Cygnus a book in an alien tongue, but that flurry faded quickly. Pat, ex-occupier of the one seat of language study at Xanthos University, knew of the extensive archeological work on Old Earth which had begun immediately when man accidently stumbled onto the planet of his origin. Through the bravery and the dream of one of the mutated humans who had survived Earth's nuclear agony, this work had been steadily adding to modern man's store of phrases, words, and some fragmented works of literature in the various languages of Old Earth.

It was not surprising, then, to Pat, to see, as the two men approached *Skimmer*, that they were of the usual racial type, two fine specimens, as a matter of fact, and that they seemed not in the least awed by the landing of a spaceship. They walked boldly, with longbows—yep, bows and arrows, Pat thought—in one hand, quivers with arrows slung over their left shoulders. They paused at a distance of about a hundred feet and looked at him in silence.

"I am a friend," Pat said, raising his right hand in salute. The two men shifted their longbows to their left hands, raised their right hands in return salute, and one of them spoke in a harsh, guttural language.

Pat's old interest in languages soared. This would

knock the socks off the ivory-tower eggheads back at Xanthos U.

But it would, he soon realized, be an immediate problem for him. If these people had evolved a language of their own during their thousand or more years of isolation, it might cause quite a problem in communications. *Skimmer*'s computer didn't have the kind of philology programming which, long years ago, had enabled translation of the Artunee manuscript.

Pat waved, saying, "Come closer. Friend. Come closer."

The two men came to within a few feet, looked up at him from guileless blue eyes, smiled, made that salute with the right hand again.

"I come from the United Planets," Pat said. "I come as a friend."

"*Ichsighgorben*," one of the blue-eyed men said.

They were dressed lightly for the warm climate. Their strong legs extended below a short, girdled skirt, chests were bare, feet semiwrapped in a type of sandal. The material of the skirts was rough, most probably woven from plant fiber.

"My name is Pat Howe," Pat said, punching himself in the chest.

"*Ichsighgorben*," was the answer, the man, too, punching himself in the chest.

Bells began to ring in Pat's head. He'd been good in his field when he was a professor of philology, and one of his last big research projects had been to compile a grammar for one particular Old Earth language from the fragments of books and inscriptions unearthed in a dig on the fringe of the largest continental mass of Old Earth.

"Ah," he said, pointing to the man who had spoken. "Gorben."

The man nodded and spoke. Pat tried to identify the words he'd helped translate with the sounds coming from the blue-eyed man. It took a while. He came down out of the lock and squatted, inviting the two to join him. They hunkered down, still holding their longbows. He encouraged them to talk, nodding, smiling, putting it all together until he thought he had it. Of course, some rough rules of pronunciation can be compiled from the written language, but they *are* rough, and when he first spoke the two men cocked their heads in puzzlement.

It got easier. There were certain gutturals which gave Pat some trouble, but he soon mastered them, and then he said, "You speak an ancient tongue, friend, a language called German."

The man called Gorben looked startled. "How do you know that?"

Pat smiled and tapped one finger to his temple, saying in English, "Smart, smart joker."

Gorben looked at his companion. Both were young, physically fit. Well-developed muscles told Pat they were not unacquainted with some form of physical work. "The one who flies from the stars speaks our language."

"Yes," Pat said, and added, "Why does that surprise you?"

The silent man's face went pale then. He looked at Gorben, his mouth open, something akin to fear in his eyes. "Only the gods," he whispered.

"Yes," Gorben said.

With a swiftness that startled Pat, the two young men kicked their feet backward and fell to lie on the ground before him, heads nodding. "Welcome, Honored One," Gorben said. "We pray that you come in friendship."

"I come in friendship," Pat said. He put his hand on Gorben's shoulder. "Please rise," he said. "This is unnecessary."

They rose, looking at him with awe. "Then you have come, at last?" Gorben said.

"I am here," Pat said.

"May you, Honored One, give your blessings to our *Dorchlunt*," Gorben said. "You will want to talk with our elder."

"Yes," Pat said. So they had reverted to primitivism, clinging to an antique language, space lost to them, perhaps even the memory of it, and he was being greeted as, if not a god, at least a powerful friend.

"Please come, then," Gorben said.

Pat gave the computer orders to button *Skimmer* up tight. When the outer hatch closed, Gorben and his companion jumped in nervousness, but Pat smiled and said, "It's all right. Don't worry."

A middle-aged woman was standing in the door of the nearest cabin as they approached. She wore a shapeless dress which fell to mid-thigh.

"He has come at last, Mother," Gorben shouted.

The woman's eyes went wide. She fell to the ground and began to nod her head to Pat. It was getting downright embarrassing. It was the first time he'd ever been a god, and he wasn't too fond of the idea.

The woman, mother to Gorben and probably the other young man, fell in behind them. On the way to the center of the village they accumulated others who first fell down in worship and then followed in awed silence.

From a cabin at the center of the village a white-haired, close-shaven, distinguished old man came to meet them.

"He has come, Elder," Gorben shouted jubilantly.

"Welcome, Honored One," the village elder said, bowing. It was a relief to Pat not to have the old man fall on his face and worship. "We have long awaited your coming."

"I am honored to be here, Elder," Pat said. "But perhaps I am not who you think I am. May we talk in privacy?" The elder, he reasoned, would be the wisest man in the village. Study of a primitive society might be interesting, if he had the time, but he'd come a long way to get some answers.

"Of course, Honored One," the elder said. He stepped aside and bowed, motioning with his hand for Pat to proceed him through the open doorway to the cabin. Pat took a couple of steps, and two sounds came to him at once. First, the beep of his communicator. He lifted it from his belt quickly, hearing as he did, a low moan of surprise from the crowd on the village square.

"Speak to me," he said to the computer.

"Alert, alert," the old man said. "Unidentified vessels—" And then there was silence. The crowd moaned. Pat turned and went rigid.

There, high up, hulls reflecting the afternoon sun, rode a battle fleet, ship after ship, huge dreadnaughts, cruisers, little destroyers, supply ships, auxiliaries. And even as he took a deep breath he saw a ship separate from the fleet and fall swiftly, under power. The crowd around him, including the elder, had fallen to the dirt in fear and worship.

It took only seconds. There was nothing he could do. The falling ship grew in size, showed the outlines of one of the new Greyhound Class space tugs. At least, he thought, they weren't going to blast *Skimmer*.

The Greyhound's fall slowed swiftly, the skipper stopping her not more than five feet from *Skimmer*'s squat hull, and then she was lifting, *Skimmer* enclosed in her field, while the people moaned and worshiped.

Five minutes later the tug was back in position, just a tiny, gleaming dot. And then the fleet blinked simultaneously and was gone.

"Well," Pat told himself, "it looks as if I'm going to have plenty of time to get acquainted."

"Rise, people," he shouted in German. "Arise, for those who fly to the stars have gone."

SEVEN

Pat had the position of honor at a well-made wooden table. The boards of the table did not bend, although there was enough food there to excuse them if they had. The main meat dish was roasted pig, a standard UP–type swine. It was delicious, and not surprising, for the old colony ships had taken everything needed to establish a lifestyle on a new planet. Only the vegetable dishes were different, and not all of them. There were green beans which tasted as if they had been cooked on a UP planet, and, of course, potatoes. The salad was different, spicy, tangy, and quite good.

Pat had had his private talk with the village elder, whose name was Adrian Kleeper. The talk had been quite revealing. Kleeper was a very pious man, sprinkling his talk with references not only to God, but to a hoard of gods, gods in such profusion that Pat, a monotheist and no scholar of comparative religions, was confused.

The important things that Pat learned from his talk with the elder were that the citizens of Dorchlunt, as they called their village complex *and* the planet, had never heard of the United

Planets, that they considered him to be a minor angel sent down by the fleet of angels which they'd seen, and that although their tools, weapons, and living utensils were primitive and self-made, they were not awed in the slightest by Pat's hand weapons and personal equipment.

Pat grinned wryly when he learned that he was not a god, but just an angel. Well, so fleeting is fame and honor.

Before the meal, the elder led the selected company, which included the handsome young man Gorben, in a prayer of thanksgiving. Pat counted references to at least ten deities. He recognized the names of only three, God, Allah, and Buddha, all, incidentally, different names for the same God who had come with the children of Old Earth into space. As an angel, he assumed that he would be expected to know all about the odd gods mentioned by Adrian Kleeper, so he couldn't ask questions.

Eating in silence seemed to be the custom. At last, everyone seemed to have his fill. There were no women present. Women had served the food, and women brought earthenware mugs of a very good and very potent beer after the meal, and, after taking an extended drink, the elder leaned back, burped into his hand, and smiled at Pat.

"Now, Honored One, perhaps you will give us news of the *forfarvelts*."

The ancestry worlds?

"All is well there," Pat said. Kleeper looked disappointed.

"Honored One," Gorben said, "has the time come, then?"

"It is near," Pat said. He was walking on thin ice. The banquet hall of the elder's cabin housed at least twenty of the finest specimens of mankind he'd seen in one place, all vital, handsome, strong young men except Kleeper, and even though he was in middle age, Pat would not have wanted to have to fight him hand to hand.

He had a sudden inspiration. "I have been sent, my friends, to live among you, to observe you, to determine your state of readiness."

"Ah," Kleeper said. "That is good."

So far so good, Pat thought. They were handsome, intelligent people, but they *were* primitive. He had no doubt that they had built up a fearsome list of laws and tabus. "My friends, as an inspector, perhaps you will see me do and hear me say things which, without knowledge, will seem odd to you. I ask your patience, and ask you to remember that there is purpose in all things."

That should cover any goofs, he thought.

"Ah, yes," Kleeper said. "The way of the gods are, indeed, mysterious."

As if to prove it, Pat's communicator buzzed at him. With a surge of excitement—had they released the *Skimmer*?—he thumbed it, and held it before his face, although that was unnecessary.

"Captain Howe," a male voice said, in English, "there is no haste, but when you have finished your meal, will you please make your way to the temple." It wasn't a request, it was an order.

"Ahhhhh," sighed the young men at the table.

"You are called?" asked Kleeper. "We had hoped that you would be our honored guest for a festival. The young women are working, even now."

"There is no haste," Pat said. Well, that's what the fellow had said.

"Splendid," Kleeper said, clapping his hands. All the young men rose. Gorben, apparently, had been appointed, or self-appointed, as Pat's guide and companion. He led Pat into the village square. Upon Pat's emergence from the cabin a band—odd-looking instruments, but sounding familiar, strings, drums, woodwinds, brass—began a sprightly melody and a dozen very pretty blond girls in short embroidered skirts and white blouses danced in perfect unison.

Something had been nagging at Pat. It crystallized in his mind as he sat in a place of honor and watched the dances of the girls, the semimilitary posturings of the young men. He was in a primitive village, on a primitive planet. Bread was baked in mud ovens. The cabins were heated by wood burned in a fireplace, and lit by lamps which used animal oil as a fuel. Water was drawn by windlass from a community deep well. The sanitary facilities consisted of privies built from rough, unpainted planks. And yet the people seemed to be uniformly healthy. And they were all much too uniformly beautiful. And where were the children? Only a few, not more than a half-dozen, ranging in age from a babe in arms to a young girl in her early teens, were in the square.

When the dancing ended, the impromptu festival over, Pat told Gorben that he wanted to walk. Gorben offered to accompany him. Pat nodded. They walked the road to the next village, where Pat found similar conditions. Apparently, his presence was known, for the people of the village were out en masse to bow low, some to fall on their faces in worship.

As the hour grew late, he walked with Gorben back to Gorben's village. "I will stay here tonight," he said. He'd been thinking about that voice on the communicator. If they wanted him before he chose to go to the temple, which he had suspected to be the stone building at the hub of the spokelike roads connecting the villages, they could come and get him.

He took food with the elder, and was escorted, after beer and more talk, which did little to answer any of his persistent questions, to a neatly furnished bedroom.

He awoke before dawn, awakened by movement in the house. He dressed quickly. Kleeper and Gorben were at table.

"We thought to let you sleep, Honored One," Gorben said.

It wasn't coffee they were drinking, but it had a tang, and a pleasant taste. Hen's eggs and bacon made up the main meal, with a chewy, tasty bread. And, breakfast over, one of Pat's unstated questions had an answer.

"Perhaps you will honor us," Kleeper said, having taken a carved wooden chest from a cabinet, "by distributing the morning prayer tablets."

"My honor," Pat said.

The sun was just above the horizon. All the inhabitants of the village were assembled in the square. They looked just too damned bright and cheerful for early morning, and Pat had to force himself to smile.

"One tablet each, of each individual color, to each person, Honored One," Kleeper said, as a line formed quickly in front of the low steps to the elder's cabin.

Inside the carved wooden box, five compartments held the latest in food-supplement tablets, some marked with the brand name of a Zedeian nutritional firm. And Pat recognized one of the tablets as a shotgun disease preventive, good for keeping the human system free of just about every known disease-causing organism. Mystery number one solved. The people of Dorchlunt were physically beautiful and unbelievably healthy because, each morning, they received dosages of the best preventive medicine and the finest in food supplements.

"Now, Honored One," Gorben said, when the little ceremony was over and everyone except the babe in arms had been pilled and tableted, "I imagine you will leave us."

Pat looked at him quickly to see if Gorben had been detailed to be sure he obeyed orders. The young man showed no signs of it.

"Yes, it is time I paid my respects," he said.

He walked alone through three villages toward the stone building. The people bowed, greeted him respectfully. It was a lovely morning. Although rain was unknown on Dorchlunt, there had been morning dew, and in the field alongside the road men were busy pumping water from the deep wells. A sophisticated system of irrigation ditches distributed the water to crops, which, in the year-round growing season, were at various stages of maturity.

The earthen road changed to a stone-paved avenue as he neared the temple. The grounds were well landscaped. Patches of flowering plants, some familiar, some not, made for a pleasant vista. The native trees of Dorchlunt were squat and thick of trunk, and had leathery, large leaves.

Two young men in short leather skirts, armed with well-decorated longbows, guarded the stone temple gates. The guards, Pat felt, were purely ceremonial, since anyone could step over the low wall at any point and approach the temple by walking pathways through flowering patches of vegetation.

There were no guards at the temple door. He

walked into a large room, lit by skylights, and halted. The room was at least fifty feet in width, and quite long. The walls were lined with objects obviously taken from the abandoned colony ship. Spacesuits had been stuffed with something so that they stood alone. Control panels, with buttons and switches, had been rather artfully built into the stone walls. And on the wall there were paintings, all of them in deplorable condition with flaking paint and large areas of damage. They were portraits, likenesses of people dressed in the styles of long ago, a thousand years ago.

Pat walked through an archway and was stunned by an array of sculpture along the walls. The medium was stone in various colors. An almost nude woman posed with an antique projectile hand weapon. A handsome man wore a military uniform painted on the stone statue with great skill, but with the paint fading, flaking. There was a nameplate for each statue, and upon close examination Pat saw that they were called gods. The God Schmidt. The Goddess Helga.

In a display of conspicuous waste on a planet with no surface water, a fountain bubbled and sang in the center of the second area. Pat walked around it. A man in a dark robe stood quietly in the next archway, hands folded in front of him.

"The goddess has been expecting you," he said, with respect in his voice. He turned, and Pat followed him through a door which closed behind them. Then another door, which was plated in hammered gold. The inner sanctum was windowless, light coming from one skylight and two oil lamps on columns set on either side of two "thrones." The thrones were also from the abandoned ship, the command chairs from the control bridge. They were still mounted on their swivels, and their backs were to Pat.

He glanced around. Most of the gold from the shielding of the blink generator had been utilized in the inner sanctum. The walls were armored with light metal from the ship. Silent, lifeless viewscreens had been built into the walls as decoration. Ship's instruments were grouped around the screens in neat patterns.

The priest who had led Pat into the closed throne room bowed to him, backed away, and went out, shutting the gold-clad door behind him.

"Anybody home?" Pat asked, speaking to the high backs of the command chairs. One chair began to turn. "Ha?" Pat said, for there was the quiet purr of an electric motor. In the temple, at least, there was power. And this brought a quick thought. The power source was damned well shielded, for he'd flown right over the temple in *Skimmer* and had been unable to detect anything.

The motor hummed, and the command chair turned slowly. He saw her profile first. Her hair had been swept up into a neat, shimmering, auburn mass, and the mass was topped by a diadem of gold and jewels. She was dressed in flowing royal purple, and the material was definitely not the homespun vegetable fibers of the clothing worn by the villagers.

Literally stunned by her beauty, Pat was unable to speak. The command chair turned to face him. She looked down at him with a smile which seemed to enlarge her mouth.

"Hello, Pat," she said.

He had to swallow, then moisten his lips. "Hello, Corinne."

"Now that you're here, you'll have to stay, you know."

"With you?" he asked.

"Yes," she whispered, rising, gathering her long, purple skirt in one hand to run down the steps of the throne dais toward him.

EIGHT

The purple material of Corinne's long gown was silky-smooth. It clung to her, and allowed the soft warmth of her to come through to Pat's hands. Her lips were more than he had remembered, and there was an urgency in her kiss which sent a surge of elation through him. Something of value lost, then reattained, increases in value. With her in his arms he forgot, for the moment, all that had happened between them in the past.

After a long, delicious time, she pushed him away, her small hands against his chest. "You shouldn't be here," she said.

Sanity returned to him. This small, exquisitely constructed lady had drugged him, had commandeered his ship and altered restricted computer tapes in a way which had almost cost him his ship and his license. She'd stolen Murphy's Stone. Beautiful she was, and he loved her. He knew that now, his mouth still tasting her kiss, but she had some explaining to do.

"Come," she said, taking his hand. "It wouldn't do for the priests to see their goddess being so human."

"Just what goddess are you?" he asked.

"I am Hera, Queen of Heaven, and Inana, Astarte, Isis, plus a few others."

"You'll have to introduce me," Pat said. "I don't know any of those ladies."

"That's not surprising," Corinne said, as she opened a door leading into an apartment which was well lit and furnished with modern items. "It was strange to me, too, until I read the sacred books."

"I'd like to read them."

"Perhaps you'll have the chance." She flowed toward a bar, turned. "I have only Taratwo wines."

He grinned wryly. "The last time you gave me a drink it hit me pretty hard."

"Pat, I'm sorry. That was necessary."

"I think I'd like you to start explaining now why it was," he said.

She sighed, poured two glasses of red wine, flowed to stand in front of him. "I will explain," she said. "First let me say that I'm so happy to see you. Really."

He wanted to believe. He took the glass. "No funny Zedeian drugs this time?"

"No," she said, with a sad little smile.

She was the only stimulant he needed. He didn't need the wine. He took one sip, reached out and took her glass from her hand, put the glasses on a table. She made no resistance as he pulled her into his arms. Her arms went around him and his mouth covered hers, and as the kiss deepened he felt a small, insignificant sting at the base of his neck. Her kiss deepened, but the joy of it was gone as a wave of shock and deep hurt killed his desire for her. He jerked her hands down from around his neck and forced her right hand open. The small hand syringe was cupped there. The quarter-inch injection needle showed a small drop of clear fluid at its tip.

"Oh, damn," Pat said, as weakness seemed to flow throughout his body.

"It will be all right," she said, her face no longer smiling. "Sit down, please."

He made it to a large sofa before the darkness took him.

Awareness came back to him with a rush. He felt fine. There was no fuzziness in his brain. He opened his eyes and squinted, for he was looking into a bright light on the ceiling over his head. He tried to move and discovered that he was secured quite firmly by straps. He was in a half-reclining position on a soft, comfortable couch. His shirt had been removed. There was a slight chill to the air which told him that, in addition to the electric lights, the room was climate-conditioned.

He jerked his head to the left. A man in a white smock stood beside him, looking down at him with his lips thrust out thoughtfully.

"Relax, Captain Howe," the man said. "No harm will come to you. We merely require some information."

"Where is Corinne?" He needed to talk to her, to tell her how disappointed he was by this new betrayal. And yet he was not too chagrined. It didn't really matter, did it? He felt fine. There seemed to be a glow of health and well-being in him.

The man in the white smock turned his back, walked away. Pat saw that under the smock the man wore a long, dark robe like the priest who had greeted him upon his arrival at the temple.

The man came back. "You will feel no pain," he said, as he pushed a mister against Pat's bare arm and injected something that burned only slightly through Pat's skin. The man then pulled a tall stool up beside the couch and perched there, looking down.

Ah, Pat was thinking, it was a beautiful world, and the couch was so comfortable, and how considerate of them to make him so comfortable.

"I am your friend," the man said, smiling.

"Yes."

"You are my friend. You want to help me. You want to tell me everything I want to know."

"Sure, be glad to," Pat said, filled with warmth for the man, filled with peace, and happiness.

"And you will hold nothing back," the man said, "because you want Corinne to know all, don't you?"

Such a burst of emotion in him as he thought of her. "Oh, yes," he said. He laughed. He knew everything. They were using a mind-domination drug on him, and that was so very, very illegal that it was funny.

"You are happy," the man said. "You are laughing with happiness, and you want to help us."

"I'd have done it without the illegal drug," Pat said, still laughing happily.

"I'm sure you would have," the man said, with a smile. "Now, let us begin. Tell me, Captain Howe, how you found us and tell me who knows that you are here."

Pat chuckled happily and told all. He told how Xanthos Central Control had detected Corinne's tampering with the trip tape, and how he'd wormed the truth out of the old man, and how he'd been able simply to follow the blink coordinates to Dorchlunt.

He was chortling so happily that he had to be primed to go on.

"And did you file a flight plan with Xanthos Central?"

"Heck, no," Pat said. "Couldn't, except in general. I gave them the known blink beacon, of course, and then I just said that I'd be exploring unchartered space."

"And the blink coordinates?" the man asked. "Did you file the blink coordinates for Dorchlunt?"

"No," Pat said. He laughed. "But they're on file at X&A. They have copies of the old man's tape from his self-diagnosis chamber. All they'd have to do is dig out the coordinates from that tape and they'd come right here, no problem. Simple trip once you have the right coordinates."

"In your opinion, how long will X&A wait, when you don't close your flight plan?"

"Oh, weeks and weeks, I'd say. Maybe months. I told Jeanny that I might be gone for a while. You see, I guess that I believed, deep inside, that I'd find Corinne, and that I might be staying with her."

"And so you have found her," the man said. "Now, let us begin again, Captain Howe."

He went through it again, laughing merrily, having a wonderful time with his new friend. "I imagine Jeanny might worry about me," he said. "Because of the personal relationship there—but I don't love Jeanny, I love Corinne—she might start a search for me in, oh, maybe two months. That would be my guess. She wouldn't want to mount a search for me and have me show up on Xanthos in the middle of it. So she'll wait. She knows I'm capable of taking care of myself. I got here, didn't I? I found Corinne, didn't I?" He laughed for the sheer joy of it.

"Now again," the man said.

"Hey, this isn't much fun anymore," Pat said, but he went through it again, beginning to feel tired, and as he talked there was no laughing as the tiredness grew and became bone-weariness, a heavy exhaustion which made it an effort to breathe. As he said, once more, that Jeanny probably wouldn't begin to worry about him for a month or six weeks he gave up, surrendered to the exhaustion, slept.

The couch was no longer comfortable. It was hard, and narrow. The lights had been dimmed. He ached in every bone, in every muscle. He lifted one arm, and the effort tired him, sent him back into sleep. When next he awoke he lay quietly, forced his eyes open. He was in a stone-lined room, and the room was windowless. The light came from one fixture, dimly, the fixture sunken into the rock of the ceiling. He heard someone breathing and, with a great effort, turned his head.

He lay on a narrow ledge, the stone cushioned only by a rough homespun blanket. An old man in the tunic and skirt which was Dorchlunt's costume lay on another ledge across the small room.

"Ah, young man, you are awake?"

"I think so," Pat said.

"Just in time. They will feed us soon."

Food was the last thing on Pat's mind. He struggled and finally was able to push himself into a sitting position, feet on the stone floor. "What is this place?"

"The waiting place," the old man said. He, too, sat up, ran his fingers through his graying hair. He looked at Pat with a little smile. "You are too young to be sent to Zede."

"Zede?"

"I am not complaining, mind you," the old man

said, "but there are laws. One must work and produce the required number of years before earning the reward."

"So you are here, in the waiting place, having earned your reward?" Pat asked.

"Yes." The old man mused. "Well, perhaps you did some great unusual service which merits early reward. Is that true?"

"Yes, it is true," Pat said. He was feeling a bit better. He was no longer happy, however, and he felt no friendliness at all toward the man who had injected him with an illegal mind-dominance drug. It was no consolation to him to know that he was not the first man to have been fooled and betrayed by a woman. And yet there was something inside him which could not accept Corinne as evil, as being a willing participant in whatever the hell it was that was going on on a planet where the population was beautiful, healthy, and living in primitive conditions next door to a "temple" where some well-shielded power source produced electricity. Perhaps it was hopelessly romantic of him, he was thinking, but he chose to cast Corinne in the role of victim, too. There could have been no faking the sincerity of that kiss there in the throne room, and even as she was drugging him again, she'd been kissing him with a fierce possessiveness which said to him, love, love.

"So perhaps we will go to Zede together," the old man said.

"You're looking forward to it, then?" Pat asked.

The old man looked at him strangely. "To be forever alive on the golden fields of Zede? To have all of one's desires, and be united with all those who have gone before us? Why do we work? Why do we observe the laws?"

"To live forever amid the splendors of the heavenly fields of Zede," Pat said, and the old man nodded.

"My friend," Pat said, "I will make a confession to you, since we are going to travel to Zede together. My service was in the field of the mind." He didn't know exactly how far to go with the lie. "I worked with the priests to delve into the depths of the mind. Do you understand?"

The old man was looking at him with interest. "How fortunate you are," he said. "And did you partake of the joy magic?"

Pat nodded. "There is one complication," he said. "Having experienced such joy, the mind is dulled, and the memory is blunted."

"Yes, yes, I have seen those who have experienced the joy magic."

"Since I am going to Zede," Pat said, "I would have my mind clear, my memories intact, lest I commit some sin of omission. Can you help me?"

"I will try."

"Tell me of the sacred books."

"Alas," the old man said. "I was not chosen to be a scholar. I know little of the sacred books of Fonforster."

"If you will tell me the little you know I will be grateful," Pat said.

"Well, then, when we came from the *forfarvelts*, fleeing the fury of the Beast, and the wings failed, there was left to us only the Fonforster. Even then the sacred books were ancient, printed upon paper, bound with leather to last the ages, unlike the wisdom which was lost with the angel wings. They are with us still, the ancient and sacred books of Fonforster, our sacred guide to living a life of meaning, and the wise ones, who interpret, who are entrusted with keeping the lights of Fonforster glowing, feed their souls upon the sacred writings and inform us, the people."

"Everyone goes to Zede?" Pat asked, just trying to prime the old man to keep talking.

"In his own time. You see, all the gods promise it. Even if it is not, as I have been told, spelled out in the sacred books, it was revealed, in the ancient days, to the priests. When the time is come one enters the place of waiting, and is given time to purify his soul in thought before undertaking the journey. I am told that it is a beautiful sleep, with secret-revealing dreams, and that after a little sleep we awake with the gods and those who have gone before. There food grows under the soft, sweet rains, and the gods themselves harvest and distribute it and are one with us. There we will walk hand in hand with the great Jove, and noble Osiris, and the great Jesus."

"My friend, my mind is truly in a muddle. I seem to be unable to remember the names of the gods."

The old man laughed. "You are not alone, brother. Only the wisest can remember all of them, for there are hundreds, thousands, including those who, coming first to this place of redemption and cleansing labor, become gods."

"I know Jesus," Pat said.

"Yes, a god among gods," the old man said. He smiled. "Although I am now enlightened, there was a time in my youth when I fear that I came almost to agree with the heretics, who—" He paused, and looked around nervously.

"Yes?" Pat asked.

The old man crossed himself and then performed several more movements of sacred import. "They, the heretics, said that Jesus and his father were the One God."

After a long pause, Pat asked, "How is the journey to Zede accomplished, friend?"

"On the invisible and all-powerful wings of the angels."

"As we are?"

"No, no. We have no need for this gross body. We are, in eternity, not creatures of the flesh, but of the spirit."

"Ah," Pat said. "A little sleep, and then the soul is winged off to Zede on the wings of angels?"

The old man nodded. "And thus," he said, "is the sacred number preserved."

"The sacred number?"

"The number of the people. There can never be more than twoscore past five thousand."

Pat felt a chill. Another question was answered. There was no evidence of an expanding population on Dorchlunt. His overflight had shown the area around the temple to be the only area of habitation on the planet. To keep the population stable must require rigid birth control, and the "sending to Zede" of older people. Looking back, he realized that all of the men he'd seen seemed to be of an age between late teens and no more than forty, with the single exception of the Elder, Adrian Kleeper.

"The ancestor worlds," Pat asked, when he had recovered from the chilling shock of realization. "Is there a name for them?"

"The sacred names," the old man breathed, and, in a sing song, began to chant off the names of a half-dozen Zedeian planets. Of the six he named, five had been destroyed in the Zedeian war by the UP planet reducers.

The old man clasped his hands as if in prayer, looked upward. "And the father world, the world of Fonforster, from whence came the sacred and ancient books, the treasure of the world, the treasure of Zede, the sacred writings and the god lists and the stories of their triumphs and acts."

Pat had more questions ready. He was forestalled by a sound of the door opening. A priest stood there, smiling at the old man. "Father," the priest said, "you may come with me."

A smile lit the old man's face. "It is time, then?"

"It is time," the priest said.

"My friend," the old man said, coming to Pat's cot to take his hand, "my journey begins. I'm sorry you're not going with me. Since your memory has been blunted, I'm sure the good priests will refresh it, so that you may prepare for your own journey."

Pat felt cold. He wished for his weapons, for any weapon. The old man was going to his death with a smile on his face, gladness in his heart. He rose, still a bit weak, paced the small cell. He had no doubt in his mind that he'd be next, and there seemed to be nothing he could do about it. He looked around for a weapon. There were only the two homespun blankets on the rock ledges which served as cots. Otherwise the room was bare. He was dressed in shirt, beltless pants, underwear, and the soft, comfortable slip-on shoes he favored. A shoe was not heavy enough to make a weapon. He had only his hands. He resolved to use them when they came for him. He would not submit calmly, without a struggle, to the injection, or whatever they used, to send a man into a little sleep and then on that "journey to Zede."

When the door opened he was standing with his back against the wall next to it. The door opened outward and he held his breath, waiting for a priest to step inside.

"Pat?"

That soft, throaty voice, and then she stepped into the cell, Corinne. She'd changed from the long purple gown into a neat coverall singlet, belted at the waist. He lowered his hands. She saw him, turned to him and smiled.

"I told them to bring you to me immediately when they had finished," she said. She shivered. "I did not intend to have them put you *here*."

She knew, and she accepted it. What kind of woman was she? He was looking at her with new eyes. "There was an old man here. He was being sent to Zede."

She looked down, and her face saddened. "Soon, such measures will no longer be necessary. We will be able to educate them out of their superstitions."

"Corinne, just who is 'we'?"

"Not here," she said. She turned and left the cell, and he followed. There were no guards, no priests. They came out into a stone corridor, made a turn, and were back at the apartment where she'd stabbed the syringe into his neck. Inside, she sat down. He stood facing her.

"I won't offer you a drink," she said, with a funny little grin.

"I don't think I could stand another of your drinks."

"Pat, it was necessary. We're so close now. We had to know what chance there was of your being followed here, and, knowing you, I don't think we'd have gotten the whole truth without the drugs. There's no lasting ill effect."

"As there was with the dexiapherzede?"

"I didn't know that the side effects were so terrible. I swear that to you."

"And yet you kept me pumped full of it for seven and a half days."

She looked down.

"Why didn't you just tell me you wanted to come here to Dorchlunt?"

"I wasn't sure of you, Pat. And it was so vital that I get the diamond here. I couldn't go back to Zede II with you with the diamond aboard. They would have—" She paused.

"The diamond is here?"

She nodded.

"Who are they, and what would they have done with the diamond?"

She sighed again. "Pat, it's a long story. Perhaps we had better have that drink."

"I'll do it, and I'll stay carefully beyond your reach," he said, moving to the bar to pour that very good Taratwo brandy. He sat on the arm of the sofa. She was curled into a chair, legs partially under her.

"When my brother was fifteen he went to Zede II on a government scholarship to continue his study of ancient history. He did his thesis on the Zedeian war of a thousand years ago. He was quite the young prodigy, astounding the learned professors with his skill in writing, and with his ability to retain knowledge, so they opened the archives to him, gave him free run. He discovered a government file tucked away in crates of documents which had once been classified top secret, but were then

so old that secrecy didn't matter. Most of them
were just dry statistics—the accounts of interest
about the war had long since been removed and
filed elsewhere—but my brother was, and is, a
very thorough man. He found one encoded docu-
ment and spent weeks with the computers break-
ing the code."

Pat eased himself down onto the sofa. Apparently she was going to take a long time getting up
to present-day events.

"You know the background of the Zedeian war?"

"In summary, yes."

"There's more tradition still alive on the Zede
worlds than in the rest of the UP," she said. "Their
legends are more explicit, for example. I've read
the books of Zedeian myths and legends. They
refer, not too specifically, and sometimes in fanci-
ful, symbolic language, to the original world, to
the Old Earth."

"Yes, I've heard of some of those myths. Serious
scholars discount them, because, after all, the Zede
worlds were settled by the same people who settled the original UP planets."

"But the Zedeians, at least the traditionalists,
insist that the Zede worlds were settled separately,
and only later, after thousands of years, merged
with the growing UP."

"Well, whatever," Pat said.

"The Zedeian myths state that before the nuclear war on Old Earth, Earth was split by rivalry
between two philosophies, or beliefs, or forms of
government—that part is not quite clear. The
Zedeians, even back in the dark beginnings of their
history, had a tradition of militarism. They say
that they are the descendants of the greatest race

of warriors ever produced on Old Earth, and that was the feeling that led, in part, to the war."

"Makes sense," Pat said. "Delusions of grandeur."

"Ah?" she asked, raising an eyebrow. "They had fought the vastly more populous UP to a standstill before the UP used planet reducers."

"OK, I'll concede that they're fighters," Pat said.

"And more scientific advances *still* come from the Zede worlds than from the rest put together," she said.

"I'd have to see figures on that."

"No matter. Before the UP began to use planet reducers the Zedeians had been working on a new, very powerful weapon. When it became apparent that they would have to surrender they loaded all the scientists and technicians who had been working on that weapon onto a colonization ship—"

"Ah, ha," Pat said.

"Yes. It's still there. Up there." She glanced upward. "Their mission was to lose themselves in space. They traveled, however, in a predetermined direction, the direction least likely to attract pursuit. Toward the core. That way, if, somehow, the Zedeians averted total defeat, ships could look for them, and find them. They were ordered to continue to work on the weapon, and they were very close to having it perfected. If they ironed out the last flaws in it, they were to arm the six ship's launches—"

"Six launches against the UP battle fleets?"

"—and return to rescue the Zede Empire."

"Let me do some guessing," Pat said. "They found only this one poor, barren planet. They were not too excited about it, but they'd gone just about as far toward the core as they could go. They put the ship in orbit and continued to work on the weapon, and one of the experiments, or something, went wrong, disabling the ship, leaving them no choice but to land on the planet and make the best of it."

Corinne nodded. "You've seen this world. It does not have the capacity to support a normal population, and the Zedeian scientists had few resources. It takes numbers, large numbers, to build a technological civilization. The planet would not support such numbers, so the scientists set up a system which has lasted for a thousand years. They limited population growth by birth control, at first, and then—and believe me, Pat, this is none of our doing—they had to resort to euthanasia of the old."

"Justifying it as sending the individual to his hard-earned reward, heaven on Zede. How did the priests, or the scientists, get such a hold on them?"

"All of the ship's information, all data, books, tapes, everything, was destroyed in the explosion and fire. There was left only one set of books, books on the superstitions and religions of Old Earth. There are twelve volumes, and even the present-day priests believe them to be the original volumes brought out from Old Earth. We've dated the material, however, and it's obvious that the books have been reproduced several times, because the existing ones are less than two thousand years old. However, the material seems to be authentic. My brother was ecstatic. He said they were, to his knowledge, the only surviving bit of printed material from Old Earth."

"If that's true, the scholars of the galaxy deserve to be able to study them," Pat said.

"Soon," she said. "Very soon."

"Tell me about the books."

"They were written in the language spoken by

the people of Dorchlunt. There are dates. They're meaningless to us, even when we compare them with the oral records of the mutated Earthlings. The books were first published in a year measured by predestruction Earth calendars as 1896."

"We know from our efforts on Old Earth that several calendars were used before the destruction."

"Yes, but the books are predestruction, very old, and very interesting. The author, a—I'll have to spell this—Klaus von Forster—"

"Funforster," Pat said.

"Yes. The author tells of hundreds of deities. It seems that every small segment of the human race on Old Earth had its own gods. Funforster made no judgments. He, apparently, believed in no god. He simply recorded the works and the word and the sacred writings of the various gods. The scientists used the books to create a code of laws and behavior. The books gave them sacred authority, for why else had they been saved from burning on the ship?"

"May I see the books?"

"Yes, of course. Later. There is much more to tell."

"Before you begin, I'd like to know the source of this power." He indicated the lights.

"It comes from a nuclear reactor," she said.

Pat's eyes narrowed. "My God," he said.

"Didn't you know that the excuse the UP used for destroying planets was that the Zedeians were using nuclear weapons?"

"I've probably read it, yes." A thought came to him. "Your brother—did he also discover directions on how to make nuclear weapons? And has someone tested nuclear weapons within the past decade or so?"

"We have no need of nuclear weapons," she said. "The Zedeian weapon is far more final in results."

"So is a planet reducer."

"A planet reducer will be useless against our weapon."

Pat whistled. "Tell me about the weapon."

"Not just yet," she said. "You asked about the power source here. The colonization ship had a nuclear reactor aboard, a very advanced one which created more fuel than it burned. They had not, in those days, perfected the techniques of drawing ship's power from the blink generator."

"But not all ships had nuclear reactors. They used solar power."

"The reactor was more efficient, and had the advantage of being transferable to a planet, if a planet was found."

"You're telling me that the Zedeians built a reactor which would last a thousand years?"

"Yes, with alterations and repairs, of course. The scientists, upon landing here, began immediately to transcribe the scientific knowledge necessary to keep the reactor in operation, and to continue work on the weapon. With all other knowledge lost, or irrelevant to the main mission, and with resources scant, all aspects of life except technical skills were allowed to revert to a mode which suited the environment. You have a curious mixture in the average Dorchlunt man. All those strong young men in the villages know how to chop wood and plant crops and harvest them by hand, but put a set of test instruments and tools in their hands and they become superb technicians. Quite a few of them can recite the most complex functions of physical law by heart, yet they can't write."

"Who is furnishing them with modern food supplements and preventive-medicine tablets?"

"That's a new thing. It's merely a precaution. When my brother found this planet, they were as healthy and sturdy as they are now. But just in case we had brought a few disease organisms with us, we began to distribute what they call the prayer tablets."

"So your brother found the ship and the planet?"

"He had trouble organizing the expedition. We weren't rich. In fact, we were poor. Our father was a hard-scrabble miner—"

"On Taratwo?"

"Yes. It was my brother's scholastic accomplishments which finally convinced the government that there was great potential gain in finding that old Zedeian ship."

"I can't resist anticipating what happened," Pat said.

She smiled and held up one hand, asking for patience. "I'm almost finished."

"Go on, then," Pat said.

"When my brother arrived here the priests thought that he was from Zede, and that he'd come to deliver them from their long exile. He was treated as a god, and he immediately saw the potential of his status. He was shown the weapon, and saw that it was powerful, but that it had weaknesses. The triggering mechanism for the molecular reaction inside the weapon had come from the resonance of excited carbon molecules. The scientists here had used a form of pressed carbon, and it took a huge mass of it to do the job. That made the mass of the weapon too large to be mounted on anything smaller than a battlecruiser. My brother grasped the theory and realized that the weapon could be made small and, moreover, more effective, by using—"

"A diamond, set to resonating by, maybe, a laser," Pat said. "Murphy's Stone."

"A diamond," Corinne said, "but my brother had no way of smuggling out enough diamonds of the proper size to provide one exciter per weapon. A bit of experimentation proved that the larger the diamond, the greater the forces generated, and that the excitation impulses could be broadcast from a central point. Murphy's Stone happened to be just the right size to be used on my brother's flagship to provide the triggering impulse for the entire fleet."

"So the Zede worlds," Pat said, "have never forgotten the lost war, are going to conquer the galaxy with a weapon better than a planet reducer?"

"No," she said, shaking her head, "not the Zede Worlds."

"Who, then?"

"The Brendens. Taratwo."

He didn't catch that use of the name Brenden in the plural at that moment. He was stunned by the ambition of the Man, of that tinpot dictator of a pissant world far out in the periphery of the galaxy.

"But why all the cloak-and-dagger to get the big diamond off Taratwo?" he asked.

"The agents of Zede are everywhere on our planet," she said. "We have identified many of them, and allow them to continue to spy on us, being very careful not to allow them to learn anything important. It has been necessary for us to cooperate with the Zedeians in order to obtain credit for the fleet we need. We had to hint at many things to get their interest—a new and all-powerful weapon, for example. That secret was safe, being known only here on this world. A spy, however, somehow learned that a sizable diamond had been found on Taratwo. The Zedeians demanded it as part payment on our debt, and, as you recall, we just barely escaped with it."

"Let's get back to the weapon. Tell me about it."

"Not yet, not just now." She rose and came to stand before him, reaching for his hands. "Pat, I've told my brother that I'm in love with you. I've promised him that you'll choose to join us. We can certainly use you. We're short of experienced spacemen. I've misused you, and I've lied to you, but I'm not lying now. It will be wonderful when we've freed the entire populated galaxy, when we've eliminated all need, and hunger, and government tyranny. Be with me, please, Pat?"

His mind was whirling. "Corinne, there's no hunger in this galaxy. We draw on the resources and industry and agriculture of over five thousand planets. No one goes hungry. There's more work than there are workers. Oh, you have those few who won't work, under any circumstances, but even they are fed, and housed, and given good medical treatment."

"There is hunger and need on Taratwo," she said, her lips compressing.

"It is Taratwo that chooses to be independent. As a part of the UP—"

"We'd give up our freedom," she said, her voice no longer soft. "We'd bow down to those who tell us what we can and cannot do, how we can live and how we cannot live, where we can go and where we cannot go."

"Honey, there have to be rules in any civilized society. I don't find the UP repressive."

"Fool," she spat, whirling away. "And I promised the Brenden."

It registered then. He rose, went to her. She did not respond when he put his hands on her arms from behind. "The Brenden is your brother?"

"Of course," she said.

"And together you're going to wipe out the fleets of the UP, the Zedeian worlds included?"

She jerked away and faced him, eyes blazing. "It was the Zedeians who almost killed us when we were leaving Taratwo," she said.

"Why?"

"Because, dammit, we'd been infiltrated. There were traitors in the space service, too, enough to seize two cruisers and try to kill us, to seize the diamond before I could bring it here."

Pat had to take time to think. He turned, picked up his drink. "Corinne, I take it that the time is near. That fleet, the one that sent down the tug to pick up the *Skimmer*, that's the Taratwo battle fleet, isn't it? And you're almost ready."

"Yes." Her mood changed, and she came to him, looked up into his eyes. "Be with me, Pat. The Brenden has said we can be married." She put her arms around him and spoke with great intensity. "You can help make it a better galaxy, darling. You can be my prince, my king if my brother dies before you. We can wipe out all the wrongs, give every man his share, his due."

It was Pat's turn to lie. Perhaps she and her brother were both mad. It was difficult to believe that the people of the original colony ship had developed a weapon which would allow Taratwo's tiny fleet to best the combined fleets of the UP. Before he made any decision, he had to see that weapon, had to know its true potential.

"Honey," he said, drawing her close, "I'm half-way convinced. I don't think things are bad enough in the UP to warrant such actions as you and your brother are contemplating, but I know this. I want to be with you, regardless."

She kissed him, quickly. "Wonderful. I'm so happy, Pat. So happy."

Suddenly, she was all business again. "My brother will be here within the week. In the meantime, I think you'll want to look over our plans, give me your opinion on the readiness of the fleet. You can be so much help, Pat, and we'll be together."

He was almost convinced, and then he remembered his brief time on Taratwo. People there had been afraid to speak of the dictator, much less to speak ill of him. The security police had had no compunction in gunning down an old miner. If that was a sample of the enlightened freedom which Corinne and her brother planned to bring to the galaxy, he wanted no part of it.

"One more question, honey," he said. "Why were you working on Zede II?"

She smiled. "You thought, at first, that I was an agent of Zede II, didn't you? You thought that I had been sent to Taratwo to get something from Brenden. Well, so did *they*, so did the Zedeians. They thought I was their agent, and what they wanted was the Brenden's jewels. Pat, Taratwo is the richest diamond planet in the galaxy. We have enough diamonds stored to decorate every fancy lady on every world. And the Zedeians had heard rumors. They wanted diamonds. What they didn't know was that I was a Brenden, that I was on Zede to influence them into trade, into trading ships and weapons for emeralds and rubies."

"Smart," Pat said, with a little feeling of unease.

"How'd you keep it quiet that there were diamonds on Taratwo?"

"The government monopoly controlled all of the good diamond sources. We developed a surefire way of locating such areas. Now and then an independent would find a few diamonds, but they were usually purchased by the monopoly. Those few that slipped past went unnoticed."

"And Murphy's Stone?"

"I told you the truth about that. The old man came to me, thinking that my greed would influence me into helping him get the diamond off the planet."

"And you knew he was going to be killed. The security police didn't have detection instruments to see Murphy in the ashfall—you told them he was going to be there."

"Pat, he had to die. The secret of such a diamond could not be allowed to get back to Zede. They had the power. We owe them billions. The UP would not have raised a hand had the Zedeians sent a fleet to collect the debt, to take over."

Well, old Murphy, Pat was thinking, so your death wasn't just an unlucky accident after all. Rest in peace.

Can a man ever know a woman? This one. She was the most beautiful woman in the world. God help him, he was still in love with her, and she'd called for the death of an old boonie rat as if by routine, all in the name of the cause. Goddam all people with a cause, he was thinking. For twenty centuries the populated galaxy had been advancing, always pushing outward, just as if, as some thought, man's purpose was to dominate all of it, the entire universe, first the Milky Way and then the other numberless galaxies which stretched outward into the unknown. For a thousand years that mass madness of humanity, war, had been under control, and now this slight, beautiful, shapely, desirable, deadly girl was going to bring back the madness.

She saw his expression change, and mistook his intent.

"You *are* with me," she whispered, smiling happily.

"All the way," he said.

Before she, herself, broke off the heated kisses which almost led to other things, he had begun to wonder if, after all, she wouldn't be worth it. With her in his arms he had all he wanted out of the universe, but if she came with power, riches, and all the goodies, wouldn't that be permissible?

NINE

Corinne was busy. Doing what, Pat didn't ask. He had the freedom of the temple. His first stop was a shielded, armored room in which rested one museum case with a set of ancient, leather-covered books, real books, enclosed in climate-controlled glass and resting on velvet. A priest went through a complicated ritual before opening the case. Pat had no hope of being able to read all the books, all the thick volumes. He picked up the first.

The language was German, ponderous, careful, exacting.

"From the beginning," Klaus von Forster had written, far away and back into the dimness of time, "man, at the mercy of the elements and the mysteries of the world, sought reassurance, something to prove that his life was no mere accident, that his existence had meaning beyond meeting the day to day needs of his body. It was, perhaps, the elements themselves which first awoke in man the need to recognize a power greater than himself."

Pat put the book down. Such thinking was still current at the coffee table of undergraduates at Xanthos U. "In the beginning," the young ones said, "man created God." And one not quite so daring might say, "If there were no God, man would have had to invent him."

Pat picked passages at random from the various volumes. Interesting, very, very interesting. The scholars at the university would bury themselves in these books for decades, for in the ponderous words of von Forster, in the history of religion on Old Earth, were hints of information which was new and dazzling. If von Forster could be trusted, Earth had had a rich and long history before the destruction, with fragmented and isolated segments of the population reaching for modern civilization at different times, in different areas.

Von Forster would be a feast for the scholar, and there was no doubt in Pat's mind that the information which the man had written to explain the social basis for the various religions and cults and gods and goddesses would give man his deepest look into his forgotten past.

But that could, perhaps, come later.

He had Corinne's permission to go anywhere within the temple complex. It was just a matter of exploration. The word had obviously been passed to the priests who presided over the functions of the temple, for he was never stopped, never questioned. When he discovered an elevator which only went down, he felt tendrils of excitement. He pushed the button. The car came up, the door opened, and going into the car, he saw that there was but one floor below ground level. The elevator opened into a cavernous chamber, crowded with equipment, test benches, people.

He wandered around idly, being nodded to by the "priests" working at various tasks. To him, a lot of the work going on looked like humbug, for

some of the priests were working with native produce and vegetation, testing various chemical re-
actions. His opinion was confirmed when one busy
priest told him that for twenty years he'd been
working with a particularly hardy native thorn
bush, feeding it variously treated extracts of po-
tato pulp in order to influence it to produce edible
fruit.

But behind a shielded door, deep under the earth,
white-smocked young men monitored the hundreds
of instruments of the nuclear reactor, and they, at
least, knew what they were doing.

He saw no odd, deadly weapon. He did not get
his first hint of it until he discovered an almost
hidden doorway and went through a sound lock
into the bedlam of excited young voices and an
odd hissing of power followed by low claps of
thunder. He rounded another baffle and saw a
dozen young men seated in command chairs, something very much like his own fire-control helmet
on their heads. At the far end of the chamber there
was swift movement and he saw a small, perfectly
outlined UP battle cruiser flash across the wall,
quickly realized that it was a holo image, saw it
shudder as a great shout went up from the young
men.

The next target, for target practice it was, was
marked with the autonomous flag of the Zede systems, and that cruiser was blasted—the low thunder was artificial and came from speakers mounted
near the target area—by his young friend Gorben,
occupying the command chair closest to him. He
walked over to stand behind Gorben.

"Honored One," Gorben said, "we are indeed
blessed that you come to watch our schooling."

"Carry on," Pat said.

"I shall blast an enemy ship especially for you, Honored One," Gorben said.

A UP destroyer zoomed toward them out of the distance, and with incredible swiftness and dexterity Gorben brought the snout of his weapon to bear and caught the destroyer in a looping evasive turn. The low thunder came as the image of the destroyer glowed.

"And thus perish all followers of the Anti-Christ," Gorben said.

"You're pretty good with that thing," Pat said.

"Honored One, I am the cadet leader, thus honored for my studious concentration and my luck with the Devil Destroyer."

"Congratulations," Pat said. "Keep up the good work, Gorben."

They were all good, all the young men. And the fire-direction controls were the latest available. All Gorben had to do was direct his eyes and his thoughts to the target and the odd-looking short-snouted weapon swiveled with a hum of gears, the snout moving almost faster than the eye could follow. Pat suspected that the entire setup was nothing more than a simulator. If the weapons had been putting out any kind of beam, or charge, the solid stone wall behind the target area would have been affected, possibly reflecting the force back toward the men behind the weapons. However, it was a highly effective simulator, with the target ships being in scale to the distances at which a battle in space would be fought at laser range.

Pat watched until a priest called a halt to the firing practice, dismissed one group of young men, and while they stood around, chattering excitedly about the exercise, seated another group behind the weapons. Pat walked toward the exit with Gorben.

"Will you be with us, Honored One?" Gorben asked.

"I'm not sure yet," Pat said.

"You shouldn't miss it, Honored One. What a glorious moment it will be when we destroy all the minions of the evil satans and demons and are, ourselves, returned to power and the glory which was once ours, through our godly ancestors."

"You are expert with the weapon," Pat said, fishing for information. "Do you know how it functions?"

"Honored One," Gorben said, "I can take the Devil Destroyer apart piece by piece and reassemble it with my eyes hidden."

"Good, very good. Can you also repair and maintain the power source?" He was still fishing. Obviously, such a weapon had to have a power source.

"I am not schooled in that phase," Gorben said. "I know, however, that the power source came with our godly ancestors, and that the secret is contained within the shell in the form of minute magic writings on thin wafers of magic. It is what happens within the Devil Destroyer itself which is in my field of schooling."

The other young men in Gorben's group had hurried on, eager to be outside in the pleasant climate of Dorchlunt. Pat and Gorben walked down a long corridor toward the exit alone.

"Let's test your schooling, young man," Pat said. "Recite to me your lessons regarding the Devil Destroyer."

"Sir," Gorben said briskly, coming to a halt, standing at attention. He began to rattle off subatomic data, most of which was beyond Pat's understanding. He knew enough of the theory to be amazed that the scientists of Zede had been so advanced in the field over a thousand years ago.

"Very good," Pat said, wishing that he'd been able to record Gorben's recitation. "Now here's another exercise, Gorben. As you know, we will soon be going back to the glory of Zede, where we will encounter people not so advanced as we. Let's imagine that we have been returned to our glory, and that a new ally, a new friend who does not understand your learning, asks you just how the Devil Destroyer works. What would you tell him, in nontechnical language?"

"This imagined friend does not know the magic words?"

"No. He is unschooled in the magic."

"Ah," Gorben said. "That is difficult."

"We will imagine that I am that person, and I will ask you questions. First, what is the source of the Devil Destroyer's power?'

"Sir," Gorben said, "the final emission of devil-destroying purity originates from two sources of power. One, the primary power source, can be driven in several ways, by solar heat, by electricity generated by a nuclear reactor, or by the auxiliary power systems of a ship. The primary power source provides accelerated-particle energy to tap the secondary power source, which is mounted in the Devil Destroyer itself. Calling the power source in the Devil Destroyer secondary is somewhat misleading, since it is there, in the closed system, that the particles are accelerated to multiples of the speed of light—"

"Whoa," Pat said. "Can you explain that to me?"

"Honored One, I thought I was explaining."

"Yes, but I'm that imagined man who knows

nothing about—what was it you said, the closed system?"

"Sir, the magic bullets which make up the atom are caught and held, ever accelerating, in a closed system—" He paused, and his brow wrinkled in concentration. "As if going around in circles, unable to escape until released by the discharge of the Devil Destroyer—" He paused again. He knew his lessons well, but to put them into nonscientific language was beyond his ability.

"How is it possible to have both the power and the space to accelerate subatomic particles in so confined an area?" Pat asked.

"Ah, Honored One, that is the magic of the god Sargoff, who first tapped the binding energy of the copper molecule."

Ah, now he was getting somewhere. Ever since X&A's one risky venture into intergalactic space had resulted in the discovery of the dead Artunee civilization and the one relic, a book in the Artunee language, UP scientists had been wrestling unsuccessfully with a theory of a new power source of such potential destructiveness that it made a planet reducer look like a child's toy. The Artunee, or so the book said, had discovered how to release the binding energy of the copper molecule.

He obviously needed more information. If the Zede scientists had actually solved the Artunee secret a few hundred years before X&A even brought back the manuscript from the colliding galaxies in Cygnus, he'd need to get a warning, somehow, back to a UP planet.

Further questioning of Gorben produced no more results. The boy simply had no way of expressing himself outside the rote of his schooling. However, Pat did learn one tidbit of doubtful utility. Grasping at straws, Pat had asked, "But why are the men of Dorchlunt the only operators of the Devil Destroyers?"

Gorben beamed proudly. "It is our schooling, sir. We are schooled on the Devil Destroyers from childhood, as were our fathers and their fathers before them. Only we have the necessary skills, sir."

"What skills are required?" Pat asked.

Gorben searched for words. "It is difficult to explain, sir. Only we can smell the exact moment of full potential."

Pat was at a loss. "You smell with your nose when the weapon is ready to be fired?"

"Not with the nose, sir, with all the senses. We smell it with our hands, our bellies, our—"

"Do you feel something, some charge, some indication of power?"

"You can say that, sir. Yes, we smell, feel, sense, I can't explain."

"And why is this important?"

Gorben's face was serious. "Should the closed system be allowed to accelerate beyond capacity, sir, the results would be disastrous."

"Explosion?"

"The Devil Destroyer would overflow and release its purity in the immediate area of the Devil Destroyer itself, and we would feel its purity instead of the satans."

Pat had more questions, but two priests came walking casually toward them, looking at Gorben questioningly.

"Honored One," Gorben said, "I am supposed to leave the temple immediately upon the completion of my schooling."

"Go, then," Pat said. "Keep up the good work."

Pat wished for a good book on theoretical physics, or the use of *Skimmer*'s library for an hour. On the surface of it, the weapon Gorben called the Devil Destroyer was just another beam weapon. Perhaps it was more powerful, but it didn't make sense that any beam weapon would be overwhelming enough to justify Corinne's sincere belief that the Brenden's small fleet could take on and destroy the UP.

He started back toward Corinne's private apartment, took a corridor that he had not walked before, discovered a golden door. The door was locked. As he tried to open it a priest came around the corner of the corridor and nodded, then halted.

"Sir," the priest said, "that is the private sanctuary of the adepts. Respectfully, sir, I must tell you that no one other than those who have taken the sacred oath are allowed inside."

"Thank you," Pat said.

"I was seeking you, sir," the priest said. "The goddess requires your presence in the rear garden."

The priest led Pat to an exit at the rear of the temple. The *Skimmer*, grand old squatting, squarish space tug that she was, sat in an open area past the flowering garden. Corinne stood beside it, waiting.

"I thought you'd be more comfortable on your own ship," she said.

"Where are we going?"

"There is a test I think you should witness," she said.

Once aboard, she gave him coordinates for a short blink, which he executed after taking the ship up a few thousand feet on thrusters.

Brenden's fleet, two thousand ships strong, lay in close formation in open space, Dorchlunt's sun on the left flank of the formation. Corinne established contact, spoke softly into the communicator, then directed Pat to put *Skimmer* below and sunward of the fleet.

"The old cruiser, there at the front of the formation, is unmanned," Corinne said. "There are only test animals aboard."

As she spoke, the cruiser's flux engines came to life, sending a glow from the thrusters. The ship accelerated quickly away from the vanguard of the fleet.

"Only the flagship will fire," Corinne said. The flagship, on the point, was a sleek new dreadnaught.

The target ship was getting almost beyond visibility and nothing had happened, and then, for one brief moment, the old cruiser seemed to glow. The glow disappeared and nothing was changed. The cruiser sped on, detectable now only by ship's instruments.

"Cory," said a voice on *Skimmer*'s communicator, "let's see if that man of yours can fly. Go latch on to that cruiser and stop it and wait until I get there."

"Will do," Corinne said. She nodded to Pat. He put *Skimmer* into motion. She hadn't done a tug job in a long time, but the program was still there in the computer. It didn't take long to catch up with the cruiser, utilizing one quick blink, and then the old man eased the *Skimmer* alongside the ship until the hulls were almost touching, enclosed the cruiser in *Skimmer*'s powerful field, and decelerated. The flagship emerged quite close, using the mass of the two ships as a target for a close blink, and two men in space gear emerged from a lock.

Pat stayed on the bridge, keeping an eye on things, using the time to scan the cruiser. The ship gave no more indication of life, or of activated machinery, than had the long-abandoned colony ship which swam its eternal orbit around Dorchlunt.

A mountain of a man with hair the same color as Corinne's came onto the bridge first, having shed his space gear. He was resplendent in a uniform which was very similar to that of an X&A Admiral. Another man in uniform followed him.

The red-haired giant studied Pat for a moment. "By God, Cory," he said, "you found yourself a handsome one, but is he a fighter?"

"He handled those two renegade cruisers," Corinne said.

Pat felt as if someone were talking about him in his absence. But then Corinne looked at him and winked. "Pat, this is my very big brother, the Brenden."

Do you shake hands with a dictator? Pat wondered. Brenden solved the problem, lumbering forward, hand outthrust, and there was no childish squeezing contest, just firm contact, with Brenden's green eyes boring into his.

"Pat, is it?" Pat nodded. "I hope you soon bed this wench, Pat. It'll damn well take some of the sharp edges off her tongue."

"Brenden," Corinne said, blushing.

"By God," Brenden roared, laughing, "if she weren't my sister and I didn't know her I wouldn't believe she's been living on Zede all these years, movie star and all, and virginity still intact. But I do know her, and I remember how even when she was a little girl she was always saying that she was never going to love a man until she found the right one, if you know what I mean."

"He knows what you mean, loudmouth," Corinne said.

Brenden laughed, then sobered. "Well, Pat, I understand you're with us. You've had fleet experience?"

"No," Pat said. Do you say "sir" to a dictator who has ambitions to rule the galaxy?

"Too bad," Brenden said, "but we'll find a place for you. You can fly, I saw that." He grinned. "And I reckon you've already scanned the target ship?"

"She's dead in space," Pat said.

"Yep. Let's suit up and go take a look," Brenden said, turning with an agility surprising in one so large.

In the corridors of the cruiser there was an odd smell, a rank, hot smell. "Pat," Brenden said over his shoulder, as he led the way, "winning the battle is just the beginning. I don't think we'll have to kill all of them. I think they'll see the light after the first two or three engagements, and then there'll be just a few of us to run one helluva big empire. I'm gonna need good men. I trust Cory's judgment, because when I first started to claw my way up from that hard-scrabble mining claim in the boonies on Taratwo she was right there beside me, clawing and scratching right along with me. Only person in the world who can hold her own with me in a fair fight, boy. Don't ever get her riled. She'll use all them ancient trick things on you and kick you in the balls, too."

"I haven't seen that side of her," Pat said, grinning at Corinne.

"See that you don't," Brenden said. "Yep, she's a fighter. No fear at all, and willing to do what it takes. Made no fuss at all when I said she'd be of the most service to us under a name other than Brenden out there on that Zede planet snowing the big dogs. Way I got it figured, Pat, Cory's my partner, and half of everything I have is hers, and that's a chunk, or will be very soon. You're her man—" He halted, turned. "Cory, why in hell didn't you marry him down there on Dorchlunt? God knows you had enough priests and a few hundred gods to swear to." He roared with laughter.

Brenden was still chuckling when they reached a squadroom. In cages lay dead animals, pigs, goats, a dog.

The other man in uniform, who had not spoken a word, pulled testing instruments from his bag and opened the cage of the dog, did some checking, and then looked up. "Dead," he said.

"Not a mark on 'em," Brenden said. "The UP eggheads will have fun trying to figure out what hit 'em."

There was a feeling of lifelessness about the cruiser. The air was beginning to stale, with the circulators off, and that rank, heavy smell was everywhere. On the bridge all the little clicking, moving, purring things had been stilled.

Brenden ripped a panel off with his hands, jerking screws loose, to expose a fused tangle of wiring. That seemed to be the source of the heavy smell. "You'll find every piece of active wiring looks the same as this, Pat," Brenden said. "And there'd be something almost as messy inside the nerve sheaths of the animals."

"Heat?" Pat asked, very much impressed, impressed to the point of being sick to his stomach to think of that weapon being aimed at a ship with a full crew of men.

"Naw," Brenden said, "fancier than that. I call it the disrupter. Dunno why. Ain't very scientific, that name."

"Brenden, why must you try to sound like a boonie rat?" Corinne asked.

Brenden grinned. "See what I mean by sharp edges on her tongue?" He made a mock bow to his sister. "The name "disrupter" *isn't* scientific, but it is descriptive. When the beam hits it stops the flow of electrons instantly in any electronic equipment. Then it sort of beats them together, and this in what happens. Since there's a minute electrical current flowing in the human body, zap. The heart, the brain, all of it stops at once."

Pat was silent. Corinne was looking at him musingly. Brenden saw the look and misinterpreted it. "By God," he yelled, "let's go down to the temple and have us a wedding."

"The wedding will be on Taratwo," Corinne said, with a soft smile, her eyes locked on Pat's "and it will be after it's all over."

"Well, it's your wedding," Brenden said. He put his hand on Corinne's shoulder. "We're ready, little sister. It's time to get your blond supermen all painted up in their warpaint and hold us one big practice drill and then go off to kick us a little sand."

TEN

Since the Brenden preferred the comfort of his flagship, Pat and Corinne took *Skimmer* back to Dorchlunt. Corinne was beaming. The test had gone beautifully. The man she'd chosen to love was with her. She was full of dreams, and she expounded on them during the short trip. They would choose one of the more beautiful UP planets for their own private kingdom. Pat would be her coregent.

"Our people will adore us," she said. "People do love pomp and splendor."

"I thought the idea was to bring freedom and equality to all," Pat said, with a little smile.

"Oh, of course," she said, "but there must be an authority figure. The masses must have a leader, or anarchy is the result."

Beautiful as she was, she could not have held her own in a freshman political discussion at the university. She paid lip service to the rights of the masses, and could weep tears for the hungry and downtrodden that she imagined to be everywhere in the UP system, basing her opinion, obviously, on conditions under the Man's dictatorship on Taratwo, but underneath it was simple ambition.

Like most revolutionaries recorded by history, she had great plans for tearing down a working system, almost none for improving it, assuming that once she and her brother were in power all things would automatically be better.

He was pleased to see that he had, apparently, gained her full trust. He landed *Skimmer* in the back garden and went with her to her apartment. The ship was still there as he looked over his shoulder upon entering the temple. He began to think of ways he could get aboard and blink to hell out of there to warn the UP to keep all ships far away from the Brenden's fleet until someone could come up with a countermeasure for the disrupter. With all of the Taratwo fleet close in to the planet, he didn't think much of his chances of doing that, but he had to try something.

At the door of her apartment, she kissed him. "Darling, I have so much to do. We'll be together forever soon, but now you'll have to excuse me."

"I'd like to use *Skimmer*'s library," he said. "OK?"

She looked at him piercingly. "I don't want to lose you."

He laughed. "I won't try to run through the whole fleet. Two cruisers, maybe, but not the entire fleet."

"I know I can trust you," she said.

"There's one other thing. There's a golden door. A priest told me that it was for adepts only, that I was barred."

"Not worth consideration," she said. "It's just the shrine to the admiral who was in command of the colonization ship. There's a statue of him. The priests worship him, keep his uniform clean and replace it as it decays, because he was the one who began the priesthood. He figured out the theocracy

which has kept these poor creatures docile for so
long." She laughed. "It's one of those arcane little
secrets that religious people love. Since all of the
original priests were sworn to secrecy as to the
purpose of the theocracy, they've extended that
secrecy to silly length." She leaned close, whispering. "The name of the fleet admiral is so sacred, so secret, that only the priesthood knows it,
and it can only be pronounced within the confines
of the shrine."

"Well, I guess I can live without seeing the
shrine," he said. "When will you be finished with
your work?"

"Give me at least three hours, darling. Then
come to me and we'll dine together." She stood on
tiptoe to kiss him again. "Are you going to try to
puzzle out all the secrets of the weapon by con-
sulting your library?"

"Well, I'm curious, of course."

"When I have the time I'll tell you all about it,"
she said. "Those old Zedeians were ingenious men.
Isn't it delightful that we're going to beat them
with their own weapon?" Her face went grim. "And,
oh, how I do yearn to see the faces of those men
who treated me as if I were a child, ordering me
about, forcing me to act in vehicles which I hated."

"Three hours, then," he said.

"I'll miss you," she said, starting to close the
door.

"By the way, I think I've got the general idea of
all of it now, except for one thing. Why do you
have to depend on the Dorchlunters to fire the
weapons?"

She cast an impatient glance at her timepiece,
then looked into his eyes. "That's the only flaw left
in the weapon," she said. "It can be quite danger-

ous, turning on itself and the ship which carries it, if an attempt is made to release the energy prematurely or if one waits too long. Given time, we could computerize the controls, but we don't have time. The Zedeians were getting extremely bothersome and suspicious. My brother knew that we could not risk waiting any longer. But there's no need to be concerned. These people have lived for a thousand years under rigid discipline. The young men are taught from childhood to feel the moment of proper charge. It's not magic, it's simply a matter of day-after-day, year-after-year training to develop the awareness of the field which forms around a disrupter. There has never been an accident with a charged weapon."

"That's good to know," he said, and then she was gone.

It felt good to be back aboard *Skimmer*. He drew coffee, seated himself at the computer console. "How have you been, old man?" he asked.

"Please repeat the instruction," the computer said.

The old man was having trouble with his hearing again.

"Now don't sulk just because I've left you alone," Pat said. "I want material regarding the molecular bonding energy of copper."

"Please repeat the instruction," the computer said. Pat typed it in instead of repeating it orally. The computer gave the equivalent of a sigh, a long, purring sound, and began to search its entire memory bank. Pat stopped it, gave more specific instructions. After ten minutes he realized that the old man was in a bad way, that the ionization in his memory chambers was worse. He checked a few individual references under atomic theory, molecular energy, just about every heading he could think of, and drew only blanks.

He remembered, then, that he had the Artunee manuscript in both original and translated form in the library. He soon had it on the screen, and it took only a few minutes to locate the references and cross-references to the material included in the story of a dead alien race. He found what he wanted in a thesis written by one Alaxender of Trojan.

"It is a fundamental law that an electron at rest, in copper, exerts a force on every other electron at rest, repelling its fellows in inverse proportion to the square of the distance between them. This force is measurable, being 8.038×10^{-26} pounds."

The force, minute in regard to a single electron, is balanced by a counterforce, respresented by a proton. If the repulsion of the protons were not exactly balanced by that of the electrons, energy would be released. Alaxender of Trojan had calculated the force represented by the binding energies in two tenth-of-an-inch cubes of copper placed one inch from each other at over six hundred billion tons. If, somehow, the balance could be destroyed, releasing that energy in a controlled stream, as it was apparently released by the disrupter—

Not much work had been done in the field since the flurry of interest following the translation of the Artunee manuscript. The blink drive, the ultimate power source, fulfilled all needs. Man did not need the power of Bertt, the Artunee. Nor did he need another weapon of destruction, so interest had lagged.

It was odd, and it was shaping up to be tragic, that some forgotten Zedeian scientist, possibly one named Sargoff, a name mentioned by young Gor-

ben, had discovered Bertt's force quite independently, and centuries before the Cygnus expedition.

The disrupter worked. And he'd seen the speed
and accuracy with which the young men of Dorchlunt manned the weapons. A UP fleet, massed for
firepower, could be swept with half a dozen of the
disrupters within seconds and each ship would
then be dead in space, with all the men inside as
dead as the ship's systems

There was no questioning the real danger to all
of UP civilization. By chance, a young scholar had
rediscovered a thousand-year-old Zedeian secret.
By chance, he'd found the colonization ship and
the descendants of the original scientists. And by
chance, a small man with a big body, an engaging
laugh, and savage, unrelenting purpose was in a
position to become ruler of the entire populated
galaxy.

"Hey, Pat," a boisterous voice said from *Skimmer's* communicator. "You there, boy?"

"I'm here, sir," Pat answered. For a while he *would*
say sir to a dictator.

"You might wanta see this," the Brenden said.
"I've got all my young studs assembling on the
parade ground. Gonna give 'em one big pep talk."

"I'll be there, sir," Pat said.

The young men of Dorchlunt were marching in
company-size units on a flat, hard-packed area to
the north of the temple. The Brenden had come
down in a launch and was seated under a sun-
shade on a wooden platform. Pat joined him there.

The ranks of young men marched in perfect unison, the troops arranged by height to give perfect
symmetry to each file. Pat recognized one of the
officers bellowing out orders as his friend Gorben.

With over two thousand young men standing at

rigid attention, the Brenden used a hailer, in order
to be heard, and spoke to them of duty, honor, and
a return to their rightful glory. When he was finished a mighty cheer went up. The dictator basked
in it, smiled, laughed, waved his hands, and then
stood at attention and saluted as the men marched
off the parade ground.

"Magnificent," the Brenden said. "God, boy, what
an army. Makes me almost wish that I'd lived in
historic times when men fought each other toe to
toe and tooth to tooth, right, boy?"

"I'm more the lover type," Pat said, and that got
a huge laugh.

Brenden waved the others, all uniformed, off the
platform. "Pat," he said, "I guess by this time
you've got it all figured out, and I'll bet you can
even give me a layman's explanation of the disrupter."

"I have a very general idea," Pat said. "Has to
do, somehow, with unbalancing the forces that
bind molecules in copper."

"Hell, that's all I understand about it," Brenden
said. "You've got the idea. What I need to know,
Pat, is just how you feel about the whole deal." He
pinned Pat with that green-eyed gaze, so like Corinne's, and waited.

Pat measured his words for a moment. "Corinne
wants to take over the galaxy to feed the hungry. I
don't think that's your motivation."

Brenden roared. "She always was a bleeding
heart. Hell, Pat, I'm taking over because I *can*.
Because I got kicked around as a kid. I *was* hungry
a couple of times, not for long, because I damned
well went out and stole enough to eat. I'm taking
over because I had the guts to claw my way up
and take over one planet and if you can take over

one you can take over as many as there are. I'm taking over because I want to make a few Zede bastards crawl, and because I think that I'm just a little smarter than some and can straighten out a few things that have always bothered me." He grinned at Pat. "And because I just don't like being forced to play second fiddle to *any* man."

"Good reasons," Pat said. "You want to know if I'm with you?"

"Cory's got her heart set on you, boy."

"I know. That's why I'm here. I'll have to admit, sir—"

"Hell, boy, you're gonna be my brother-in-law, just call me Brenden."

"Thanks. I'll have to admit, Brenden, that I'm not wild about killing. I don't get all excited about blasting poor guys in UP ships."

"Neither do I, neither do I. We're gonna start slow. We'll kill only enough to make believers of the others, and of the UP politicians. Hell, Pat, I ain't no murderer, but sometimes events are bigger than individual men, you know that."

No. Pat didn't know that. He knew that the underlying philosophy of the more enlightened people in the UP confederation was just the opposite, that the rights of the individual were more important than any event, or any theory, or any belief, or any government, and the UP had been working toward total individual freedom, under a few necessary laws, for the last few thousand years.

But he nodded in agreement to Brenden's statement.

"You love my sister, don't you?"

"Yes," he said truthfully, for in spite of everything he went soft inside when he thought of Corinne.

"Well, then?"

"I'm with you, Brenden," he said, because, above all, he had to retain his freedom of movement so that he could seize whatever chance came along to try to avert the catastrophe which Brenden was planning.

"Here's my hand on it," Brenden said. And still holding Pat's hand in a firm clasp, he said, "I want you with Cory tomorrow."

"What's happening tomorrow?" Pat asked, a feeling of dread inside. Was it to be so soon?

"She hasn't given you the timetable." He laughed. "Guess you two have been too busy to talk business. Well, here's the plan. Tomorrow we have a sort of dress rehearsal. We'll split the fleet, and be targets for each other with uncharged weapons. That'll give the gunners some live onboard practice. Cory'll be in command of the second wing, me the first wing. You go with Cory. She's not too hot about being in command, and if you think you can learn enough to cut it, we'll see. I need someone I can trust."

"You can't trust the men who've been with you all along?"

"Hell, boy, we've only had a fleet on Taratwo for a few years. Haven't had time to train good navy men. I got a few I can trust with my life, but not with the command of a wing. They're good men, but they lack experience. And anyhow, my brother-in-law has to be a big part of it, doesn't he?"

"I appreciate it," Pat said.

"After the fleet exercise in space we'll have one more of these parade shindigs. I like that. And it'll be good for the boys. Keep them alert and ready. Listen, these kids are the key to it, you know. I guess you've dug up how sensitive and critical that damned weapon is."

"Yes, and that scares hell out of me," Pat said. "What if in the heat of battle one of the boys loses his nerve, or gets excited? Can you shut off the excitation impulses generated by Murphy's Stone?"

Brenden shook his head negatively. "Once that big rock is at temperature it stays that way for a while." He laughed.

"That's a chance we have to take, but nothing's going to happen. These kids have been in training all their lives. I've run psychological tests on dozens of them. They don't get nervous looking old man death right in the teeth, because they've been told all their lives that they're going to that heaven on Zede when they die. They welcome death, but, on the other hand, they don't seek it."

"When do we sally for UP territory?" Pat asked.

"OK. I didn't finish, did I? The exercise tomorrow, then a day off except for the parade for the boys, and one more final test run in space. Soon as that's over we don't even come back down, we just light out for Zede territory."

"Going to start with Zedeians, huh?"

Brenden grinned wolfishly. "You bet your ass, I wanta hear those bastards beg for mercy."

"So three days from now the final exercise in space and then we're off?" Pat asked.

"That's it."

The last of the marching units were leaving the parade ground. Brenden went to his launch. Pat followed the marching men, saw the last unit halt, come to attention, then he heard Gorben's voice dismissing them. The young men went off at the run for their villages, cheering and laughing. Gorben was walking toward Pat.

"Very impressive, Gorben," Pat said, when they were face to face. "I suppose you're ready for the big exercise tomorrow?"

"Yes, Honored One."

"What is your battle station?"

"I have the honor to be gunner on the flagship, Honored One."

"So you're at the master control, then?"

"That is my honor, sir."

Pat was searching desperately for an idea. If only he had some way of reaching Gorben, of convincing him that he had been misled. But Gorben and all the others were strong in their faith, a faith which had been built by a lifetime of indoctrination. No Dorchlunter would willingly disobey an order, or go against the plan of the redhead who was the leader of the angels of the gods who had come to lead Dorchlunt back to glory.

Pat was just one man against a fleet of over two thousand ships, each with a complement of Taratwo men aboard, plus these impressive young warriors of Dorchlunt.

"I saw you in the reviewing stand today, Honored One," Gorben said. "I was pleased that you were there."

"Thank you," Pat said.

"Your respect for us honors us," Gorben said. "I would that all the others had the good fortune to know you and to speak with you as I have."

A faint hope came to Pat, an impossible plan. "Well, we all serve the gods, Gorben."

Gorben crossed himself devoutly.

"And I serve one god in particular," Pat said. "I serve the god whose name cannot be voiced."

Gorben turned toward the temple, bowed his head quickly once, twice, three times. When he turned his eyes were wide. "I knew, Honored One, that you were of divine importance."

Pat wasn't quite sure where he was headed, didn't have it all worked out. All the odds were against him, but there was a faint, glimmering hope, that hope reinforced by Gorben's devout reaction to the mention of the god of the priesthood, the Zedeian admiral who had established the theocracy on Dorchlunt.

"Soon, my friend," he told Gorben, "we will all be able to speak the sacred name."

Gorben's eyes were wide. "*He* will be with us?"

Pat shrugged. "Who can fortell the will of the gods?"

ELEVEN

When Corinne admitted Pat to her apartment she was dressed in the misty, flowing creation of a Zedeian fashion designer. A priest served table as they ate. The conversation at table was carried by Corinne, as she asked questions to delve into Pat's past. She had to hear all about his youth on Xanthos, teasingly demanding to know if he'd fallen in love with cute little girls in first school. Lovers' talk. She had a great need to know *all* about him.

She talked a little about herself, at Pat's insistence. There were a few things he hadn't been able to put together, for example how it was possible for her to visit Taratwo as a guest holostar without people knowing she was the Brenden's sister. It was easily explained. As a young girl, she'd been farmed out as a half servant, half ward, to a well-to-do family. She'd attended school not as Corinne Brenden, but as Corinne Tower, and it had been as Corinne Tower that she rose to provincial stardom on Taratwo, and was "discovered" by a Zedeian filmmaker. But all along she and her brother corresponded, visited when they could, and when Brenden latched on to a right-wing movement, rose to leadership, and, eventually, accomplished a swift coup which made him supreme power on Taratwo, she had begun to act as his agent on Zede II.

Mostly, however, during that meal and afterward, when they danced, just the two of them alone in her apartment, she refused to talk about herself, or about coming events.

"I want this to be our night, Pat," she whispered. "Something to remember, something which I will have if anything should go wrong."

"What could go wrong?" he asked.

"You don't seriously think that we'll accomplish our goal without losses?" Now and then her green eyes could harden to a point where it seemed that they could cut glass.

"I haven't allowed myself to think about it," he said. "You could remain here."

She laughed. "No. My place is with my brother."

"He says I'm to be with you," Pat said. "That makes me feel as if I'm just extra baggage. I think I'd like to have a ship, Corinne. At least I'd be performing a useful function."

"So you want to be useful? Then kiss me," she said.

For a long time Pat did not think of the very real danger to the UP. Man's love for woman, and Pat's need for this particular woman, must have been, he thought wryly, the original mind-dominance drug, for with his lips on hers nothing else mattered.

She lay on her back on a large, soft couch. He leaned over her, torso to torso, mouth to mouth. She trembled, clung, seemed to be trying to press herself so closely to him that she became welded to his body.

When she spoke, her voice was husky and un-steady.

"I don't want to wait," she whispered.

Neither did he.

"It doesn't really matter, does it?" Her eyes were wide, and there was a touching look of desire, and perhaps just a little innocent fear, on her face. Somewhere deep down in Pat a touch of his old cynicism surfaced. Either she was the most skillful actress he'd ever known, or she was, as her brother had stated, totally inexperienced in love.

Within minutes, he realized, he would know more about *that*, for his need was great, and there was the chance that *something* might happen, because even with an overwhelming weapon the Taratwo fleet would not escape without losses. The sheer number of UP ships assured that. Was she thinking the same thing? Did she want to seize what they had, rather than risk dying without having anything?

"It matters to you," he told her, kissing her soft lips with little pecking attacks. "It is you that matters."

"Then make love to me, Pat." Her voice broke, and she closed her eyes.

He wanted to make love to her. He let his hands begin to know the smooth curves of her, thought smugly that he, old Audrey Patricia Howe, loved and was loved by the most beautiful girl in the populated galaxy. And he almost, almost, did.

Giving up Corinne Tower was the hardest thing he'd ever done. The thought process, running as an undercurrent to the wildness of his need for her, was not a logical process from A to B to C. His thoughts were chaotic. He remembered that first night aboard *Skimmer* when he saw her in the

Zede film, and the dream in which she'd come to him, and he remembered how she'd looked so beautiful even while he was drinking the drugged liquor which put him through seven and a half days of hell, and the love in her eyes even as she stabbed his neck with a syringe.

But that woman wasn't Corinne Tower, that woman was Corinne Brenden.

The two are the same. They're one. They're inseparable.

She's the most desirable woman I've ever known.

She has the political morality of a spider.

She trusts you, Pat. She trusts you. She's willing to send those naive young Dorchlunt men off to kill millions of people, but she trusts *you*, and she loves you.

He went so far as to see that her breasts were perfection. Her reaction to his kiss there was wide-eyed amazement and clinging.

For a moment, then, she was calm and self-possessed. She pushed his head away, looked at him, those green eyes piercing. "One thing is important to me," she said.

"Yes?"

"I can never prove, without your trust, that you are the first man ever to see me like this."

"I believe," he whispered.

"When you know that you are the first to have me, will you believe that no man has ever seen me?"

Well, it *was* possible. Not probable, especially considering that she'd worked in the film industry, but it was *possible*.

"Yes," he said.

Her intake of breath, her wide eyes, her trem-

blings, which could have been fear, touched him—
and then he was talking to himself again.

She trusts you, Pat, and you're just waiting for a
chance to stop this criminal thing she believes in.
And even if she's willing to kill millions, and perhaps tear down civilization as you know it, right
now she's just a girl, just a young woman who
loves you and trusts you.

"Corinne, let's talk for a minute," he said, pulling the silken material of her gown up to cover
her.

"Talk?" she asked. *"Talk?"*

"I do believe you," he said truthfully. No woman
could be that accomplished of an actress. "Brenden
said you had always been romantic, that you had
always looked forward to loving one man."

She giggled. "Someday when we have hours and
hours, I'll tell you how damned difficult that was,
the ruses I had to use."

"It was that important to you, wasn't it?"

"Of course," she said, beginning to look a bit
puzzled.

"Then it's important to me to help you keep that
resolution, Corinne." He rose, pulling away from
her clutching hands. "Honey, you've waited this
long. We can wait a little longer."

Because, although his conscience ordered him to
betray her, to do all he could to stop the Taratwo
fleet, he could not betray her on a personal level. If
he accepted her offer of herself, then he'd be bound
to her, for having accepted something which she
had valued so much, he could never, then, betray
her in any way.

"Damn," she whispered. "I told you how I feel.
This could be, I pray that it won't be, but it could
be our last time alone together before we fight."

"I know, honey, I know. You think about it, though. See if I'm not right. It will be much better this way. We'll take the old *Skimmer* after we're married and get lost in space somewhere for weeks and weeks."

She came into his arms, weeping. Her kiss relit the flames in him, but then she was pulling away, talking through tears. "I do love you so much," she sobbed, "and to think that you value me that much, are so considerate of my feelings, that makes me love you even more."

He spent the night on the *Skimmer*. Corinne joined him there early in the morning, in a neat blue uniform, all business, and they lifted up to join the fleet. Corinne's flagship was a gleaming new heavy cruiser. It had come out of a Zedeian shipyard less than one year past, and represented the latest in naval technology.

The ship's disrupter installation was topside forward. The weapon was manned by a young Dorchlunter cut from the same pattern as all the others, a serious, handsome boy of not more than eighteen. Fleet communications was handled by an officer from the Brenden's home planet, a brisk, efficient man who, under Corinne's orders, soon had her half of the fleet in formation to attack the other half of the fleet under the Brenden's command.

The last time ships of war had opened the double fail-safe locks on weapons was when a small UP fleet wiped out the pirates who had made the Hogg Moons their hideaway. And yet, with UP X&A ships opening new blink routes constantly, with the knowledge that at one time there'd been a killer race in the galaxy, ships of war and their crews needed training, just in case. The fleets of the UP were always having war games. It was standard practice for all ships, including those built for Taratwo by the Zedeians, to have a way of keeping score accurately in those war games. Each weapon was equipped with a harmless beam projector, and the ship's sensors were tuned to detect the light beam's impact, should a ship be hit. Thus there were two records, one on the ship which fired the weapon, and one on the ship which was hit. Central fire control gathered the computer data and, in a war game in space, sent out the word to victim and victor when a ship was hit.

It had been, Corinne said, fairly simple to integrate the disrupters into the system. By activating only the primary power source of a disrupter, a stream of harmless electrons bypassed the closed system of the secondary power stage and registered as a hit on the target ship.

UP naval tactics were well recorded, in hundreds of books. Since the Zedeian war, theories had not changed. A fleet was most effective when in formation, bringing massed firepower to bear. A naval engagement, then, would become a struggle of endurance, shield against laser, AMM against missile. UP tactics were perfect for the Brenden, for, unlike the UP ships, his ships had to make only one hit, on any portion of a ship, to be of deadly effect. Laser weapons, missiles, projectile weapons—all had to make multiple hits on a shielded ship to do significant damage.

Corinne chose a modified V formation. From that formation, firepower of all ships could be concentrated. The Brenden came with stacked ranks, the screen images showing a square made up of little dots, the ships stacked line on line above each other, but with the ranks falling away at staggered distances to make for differences in range for the opposing fleet.

Taratwo men manned the conventional weapons. Missiles would not be used. They were too expensive, and too easily countered with AMMs. In a real action, the main purpose of using missiles was to divert the enemy's attention, to keep a portion of his computer capacity engaged, and to keep men busy. In an exercise, missiles were simulated by computer, and the men at the AMM stations would be engaged in sending out not actual killer missiles but little electronic blips on a computer screen.

Two exercises were running simultaneously. Each half of the fleet was doing its best to make enough laser and missile and projectile hits on the other half to keep from being tagged with the electron stream from a disrupter.

The results were overkill.

Pat had gone to stand near the young Dorchlunter. Laser range and disrupter range were almost equal, so that even as Pat saw the blinkings from the Brenden's fleet, the disrupter gunner was spraying simulated death, taking out ship after ship in a display of swiftness and efficiency which was awesome. Only scattered laser hits registered on Corinne's fleet, not enough to strain the screens. The swarm of simulated missiles were engaged by a swarm of simulated AMMs from Corinne's fire control; projectile weapons were never used, for there was not time before multiple disrupter hits had left the Brenden's fleet dead in space.

The action lasted less than five minutes. It took a quarter hour for the computers to gather and tabulate. Not one ship in either fleet had been seriously damaged by conventional weapons. *Every* ship, in each fleet, had been killed, and killed again and again by the deadly, swift, emotionless gunners behind the disrupters.

The Brenden joined them on Corinne's flagship. "Makes me almost feel sorry for the poor bastards," the Brenden gloated. "I'd say it'll take just about three engagements to have them yelling for negotiations, and maybe two more after that for unconditional surrender."

"What if they change tactics?" Corinne asked.

The Brenden laughed. "Military thinking was frozen in place a thousand years ago."

"Still," Corinne said.

The big man mused. "All right, the day is young. Let's have another go at it. This time you change to any tactic you care to use."

"I'm not very imaginative in that way," she said. She smiled, brightened. "And besides, you know me too well, so well you'd be able to figure out what I was going to do in advance. Let Pat direct the fleet."

"How about it, future brother-in-law?" the Brenden asked.

Pat had been trying to think up some way of lessening the effectiveness of the disrupters. "Fine," he said. "I have got a couple of ideas I want to try out. The situation is that there have been at least two engagements, in which all UP ships were destroyed without loss to . . . us." He started to say "you," amended it just in time.

"How much time do you need?" the Brenden asked.

"Give us an hour after we withdraw to maximum detection distance," Pat said.

Pat gave his orders to the fleet communications

controller. Corinne's ships formed, started away from Dorchlunt's sun.

"How good are your pilots?" Pat asked Corinne.

"Not as quick as you, but well trained. They can follow orders," she said.

"Get me Brenden," Pat told the communicator, and when he heard the big, rowdy voice, "Brenden, I'm going to give orders to my boys on intership channel nine, in the open because we don't want to take the time to set up scramblers. Tell your ships to stay off that channel."

"Right," Brenden said.

"And no cheating," Corinne said, over Pat's shoulder.

Brenden laughed. "If I cheated that would destroy the effectiveness of the exercise," he said.

Pat went to work, giving orders to the computer operator, and to the control officer. The Brenden's fleet was just at detection distance, a distance which could be measured down to an accuracy of a few feet. He had already scouted that area of space, for Brenden had not moved from the site of the former exercise, so it was perfectly safe to blink his fleet.

It took a while to program all computers on each individual ship, to set blink coordinates, to brief the pilots and crews on what Pat expected.

On the Brenden's flagship, men were tense, not knowing exactly what to expect. The dictator was pleased, because there was a feeling of real emergency in the air, just as there would have been had that fleet out there been UP. He figured he was getting a pretty smart brother-in-law, after all, and then suddenly alarms began to clang and the ship's shield sizzled with multiple laser hits and the computers began to sing out warnings of an incoming swarm of missiles from 360 degrees.

Brenden roared with pleasure. Pat had blinked his fleet, positioning his ships in a containing sphere, and Brenden's half of the fleet was being attacked from all directions, the attacking ships so carefully positioned that misses did not strike a friendly ship but sizzled harmlessly through gaps in Pat's formation.

Brenden lost twenty ships before his cool, efficient gunners decimated Pat's fleet, leaving less than four hundred ships to blink, after an initial flurry of fire, back to safety. Brenden's fleet was hit again, and again, by the waves of simulated missiles which were still registering on his computer screens, and then, with his losses at just under one hundred ships, he sighed with relief and started to get on the communicator to congratulate Pat. He didn't have a chance to speak.

They came back, the survivors, the flagship with Pat and Corinne aboard, in a wild melee of corkscrewing, hot-dog, individual attack, the pilots yelling in delight, experiencing a freedom of action they'd never known before, slamming into the midst of the Brenden's ships and taking a toll.

Gorben, at the disrupter aboard Brenden's flagship, also acting as coordinator for the fleet gunners, was giving calm, swift orders as he jerked his weapon from target to target, taking out ship after ship, knowing that his own ship was disabled by enemy laser fire, but still alive and fighting, and then there was quiet, all ships in the attacking fleet tagged by the disrupter beams, all their men dead.

"My God, boy," Brenden roared, when he was, once more, back aboard Corinne's flagship, "where'd you get such ideas? You took out almost two hundred of my ships. Some of them can be repaired, but the computer estimates that we lost over a hundred and fifty for good, along with about fifteen hundred men."

"I just put myself in the position of a UP fleet commander," Pat said, "and wondered what I'd do if I'd lost a couple of fleets without doing any return damage. They're not stupid, Brenden. They'll adapt."

"Well, thanks to you, we'll be more ready for surprises when the real thing starts," Corinne said.

"Pat," Brenden said, "I hereby appoint you, but only temporarily, the official enemy. I want you to spend the time between now and day after tomorrow putting yourself in UP shoes. Think up some more surprises for us."

"I'll do my best," Pat said.

"Well, let's gather up the scattered chicks and head for home," Brenden said. "Oh, I want you on the reviewing stand tomorrow with us, Pat." Pat nodded.

"You did well, darling," Corinne said, when they were alone, back aboard the *Skimmer* on the pad behind the temple. He had told her that he didn't think it was a good idea for him to go to her apartment with her, that he wasn't sure his willpower would be strong enough a second time.

"Coward," she'd said.

"You bet," he had told her.

She was tired. She admitted that the strain of being in command of half the fleet drained her. She told him she was pleased that he'd be in command during the final training exercise. She was, he thought wryly, willing to give him all the battle glory, so long as she had her throne, her worlds, with him beside her.

He walked her to her apartment, kissed her, just once, and pushed her inside. Then, back on the *Skimmer*, he searched among the spare parts and tools stored in the mate's cabin until he found a small hand-held cutting tool. Time was running out, and the only plan he'd been able to come up with was a far-fetched, hare-brained one which, if it succeeded, would have some drastic effects that he didn't even want to think about. He didn't think he'd have to worry about it working, however, because it depended upon his setting the scene properly and then getting a chance to speak privately with Gorben, and if he was lucky with a few of the other Dorchlunters.

He didn't know exactly how he'd be able to manage that, but there was a step which had to be completed before he'd be in a position to talk with Gorben and the others anyhow, and if he got through that one alive he'd worry about the rest later.

TWELVE

Pat set a wake-up alarm for three a.m. He'd thought he'd have difficulty falling asleep, but he didn't even finish his drink before his eyes became heavy, and then the soft bell of the wake-up was in his ears and he was dressing.

The temple doors were never locked. He went in through the back door and made his way toward the interior. The corridors were well lit, but all was quiet. Within five minutes he stood in front of the golden door to the priests' inner sanctuary, the most secret of places, the sanctuary of the god whose name was so sacred it could not be spoken, except within the confines of the sanctuary itself.

The door had an old-fashioned lock which required a mechanical key. He used a more modern key, the small cutter he'd brought from the *Skimmer*, slicing the bolt neatly as he played the cutting beam into the small crack between door and jamb.

The priests had done all right for themselves. The sanctuary was a storehouse of treasures, of art and gold and incongruous mechanical items from the old colony ship. What he was looking for stood on a dais at the far end of the room.

There must have been, he thought, some pretty good artists aboard that old ship, for the statues in the main entry to the temple were realistic and very well done, and the statue of the god whose name couldn't be spoken aloud was still more realistic.

He stood there as if alive, in the gaudy uniform of a Zede admiral of the fleet. His name was engraved in stone on the pedestal on which he stood, Admiral Torga Bluntz.

Luck was with Pat. There were no priests in the sanctuary, no warning sensors. Strict, theocratically applied discipline had, for a thousand years, made good citizens of the Dorchlunters. There was no need to set guards, except for ceremony, as guards were used in front of the temple. His luck continued as he climbed onto the dais. The statue of the fleet admiral was life-size, and was within a half inch of Pat's height. Torga Bluntz had been a man of personal discipline, too, for, although his face, painted in lifelike color, showed the wrinkles of age, he had kept himself in condition.

The uniform in which the statue was dressed had, evidently, been renewed in the recent past. Although the material was the homespun of Dorchlunt, the insignia were of ancient metal. The coat and high-necked shirt came off the statue easily. The trousers were another matter. The statue was carved from native stone. There was no way to slip the trousers off the statue's feet. However, a bit of study showed Pat how the trousers had been put on. The back seams of the legs and pants of the trousers were basted loosely together. Pat took his fingernail trimmer and cut the threads, and then, the uniform folded neatly, made his way back to the *Skimmer*.

A bachelor is forced to develop some odd skills. Pat could handle an automatic hand-held stitcher. The seams may not have been exactly straight when he finished, but the trousers were in one piece, the legs sewn into tubes, and the flat of the seat closed, and they fit him fairly well. The high-necked shirt was a bit tight, but the coat fit comfortably. The ornate gold-braided cap fit after he put some folds of cloth at the back to make it a bit smaller. He examined himself in the mirror in his cabin and was satisfied.

He locked the uniform in his personal locker and went to sleep. The final parade of the gunners was scheduled for midday. He wouldn't have any opportunity to talk to Gorben, or any of the Dorchlunter gunners, until after the dress review. He didn't know exactly how he'd accomplish it *after* the review, other than by going into the villages to seek Gorben out. He'd have to find an excuse for that, without arousing Corinne's suspicions. He hoped that she'd be busy with whatever last-minute preparations a woman makes before going out to conquer a galaxy.

He was awakened by the ship's communicator. It sent a persistent melodic summons which, the timer told him, had been sounding for almost half a minute. He'd have to be a bit more alert than that if he ever got back into space.

The Brenden was on. "I thought maybe I'd called the wrong place," Brenden said with a chuckle. "I was just going to call Cory's apartment."

"I was sleeping in," Pat said.

"Pat, have Cory find you a uniform. You two are going to have to review the troops today. I just had a ship come in from home, and there are some details I have to handle. I should be finished by early evening. We'll all get together for a celebration before the big day."

He was gone. When he was dealing with business, the Brenden could be curt.

Pat thought about that. It was good that Brenden wasn't going to be planetside. Now all he'd have to do was sneak away from Corinne.

The review would begin in two hours. Pat had a quick snack for breakfast, then went into the temple. The priests were going about their duties, whatever they were, calmly. Apparently they had not discovered that the lock on the door of the admiral's sanctuary had been cut open and then fused back together.

He was near the corridor which led to the practice range for gunners. He wondered if any of them were there. Probably not, but he went through the working area, where priests were still trying to do wonders like make a thorn vine bear potatoes. The practice range was dark and inactive. On the way back through the work area he saw a priest packaging the tablets he recognized as the food supplements and preventive medicine given to the Dorchlunters. He paused to watch a moment.

"Good morning, sir," the priest said. He was one of the oldest Dorchlunters Pat had seen, perhaps over fifty.

"How's it going?" Pat asked.

"Well, well. The young men must have their prayer tablets when they soar away to glory."

"And is it your job to dispense the prayer tablets?"

"I have the honor to be the temple healer," the priest said.

A sneaky idea came to Pat. That the idea was not original to him made for a certain sense of justice.

"Healer," he said, "you are fortunately met." The Old Earth language made for a formality of phrase. "As it happens, I have difficulty sleeping. Perhaps you have something to help?"

"My pleasure, sir," the healer said. He walked to a cabinet and came back with a small box. "There is a measuring spoon inside, sir. For a man of your size and weight, I recommend one scoop. If that is not enough, try two, and by no means should you ever ingest more than five scoops in one night."

"Is the powder quick-acting?"

"Very quick-acting sir." He chuckled. "It might be best if you are prepared for bed before you take the powder."

Corinne was waiting for him. She was already in uniform, although there was still plenty of time to wait before going to the parade gounds. Pat suggested that there was, indeed, time for a little taste of something to give them energy for the long ceremony. He went to the bar and mixed.

"I'd just as soon call off the review," she said.

"No, I think the gunners are looking forward to it," he said.

"Yes, I'm sure you're right." She seemed slightly agitated. When he remarked on it she said, "I was thinking of what happened yesterday. You're right, Pat, they won't give up easily."

"We'll come through all right," he said. "Drink up. It'll make you feel better."

"I am so sleepy all of a sudden," she said, not ten minutes later, as she cuddled in his arms on the sofa. He smoothed her glorious auburn hair.

"Take a little nap," he said. "I'll wake you when it's time."

"Don't know why I'm so ..." she said. Then, after a long pause, she tried to say "sleepy," managed only "sleeee ..."

He carried her to her bed, covered her with a light sheet, looked down into that beautiful face which seemed so innocent. "I hope it won't give you as bad a hangover as I had the first time," he said.

He experimented with trying to wake her. Nothing, not even lifting her and shaking her, would do the job. He had just under thirty minutes before the first of the troops would begin to form on the parade ground. He went back to the *Skimmer* to make his preparations, walked around the temple, wearing a long greatcoat which was much too warm for the climate, took his place on the review stand, standing quite alone and straight, the greatcoat covering the uniform of Fleet Admiral Torga Bluntz. He would not have to find a way to sneak into the villages to talk with Gorben and a few of the others. He would have them all assembled before him within a half hour.

The handsome, well-formed, blond young men of Dorchlunt marched in company-size formations onto the field, feet moving in perfect unison, eyes snapping right as they passed the review stand, where, to their initial puzzlement, one man in a greatcoat stood to watch them. Gorben and a few of the others recognized Pat, and for Gorben it was a special thrill to know that his friend had the sole honor of the final review before glory.

The voices of the officers and the drill sergeants rang out in the still, warm air. The sound of feet in unison thudded on hard-packed ground. And then

they stood before him, two thousand strong, as
fine a group of young men as Pat had ever seen.
For a moment, terrible doubt came to him, but he
forced himself to picture a massive UP fleet dying,
and then the march of the Brenden's form of government, with its hard-eyed security police, across
the populated galaxy.

The gunners stood at attention. Pat had been
standing with his hands behind his back. He raised
one hand, placed the admiral's cap on his head,
shrugged out of the greatcoat and let it fall, and
took two steps forward.

A gasping moan of surprise came from two thousand young throats. Military stance forgotten, the
gunners made three quick bows, some of them so
confused by the sight of the god in the flesh that
they at first tried to turn to face the temple and
the god's shrine.

"Stand at ease," Pat roared.

Discipline returned. Feet moved in unison. Arms
shot behind backs.

The God Fleet Admiral Torga Bluntz, Gorben
realized with a thrill of pride, had been among
them for some time, and had actually favored him,
Gorben, with his friendship. He stood at ease, his
young chest thrust forward, his eyes adoringly upon
the resplendent figure on the stand. The God Bluntz
had returned, just as he had promised he would,
and was there to lead them back to their rightful
place in Zede and in glory. And the god had once
told him, had he not, that soon all would be able
to speak his name openly.

"Warriors of Zede," Pat said, using a hailer so
that his voice carried to the last man in the rear
ranks and reverberated into the distance. "I com-
mend you on your work, and on your readiness."

The God Bluntz had more to say, much more, and when he had finished the young gunners stood, stunned with surprise and happiness. Then, as from one throat, their voices rose to the skies in a thunderous cheer. The God Bluntz raised his hands.

"I will speak, here, with Gunner Gorben," he said.

Gorben felt that he would burst with pride as he marched to the stand.

"My friend," Pat said, moved almost to tears by the look of pride and happiness on Gorben's face, "call here the gunner who will be with me on the flagship of the goddess."

"Sir," Gorben barked. He made a precise about-face. "Gunner Werner, front and center."

A tall young man broke from the ranks and double-timed forward.

"Tell the officers," Pat said, "to move the troops and dismiss them. You two come up here with me."

The God Bluntz had special instructions for the gunners Gorben and Werner. His instructions to the troops had fired the hearts of all with gladness. His words to the two on the stand—while drill sergeants and officers bawled orders and the troops marched off—had a different effect, although both young men tried to hide it.

Pat was not proud of himself. He knew that he would always remember the almost hysterical cheer of sheer joy which two thousand young men had given him.

Nor was he proud of his actions with Corinne. When he returned to her apartment, after stowing the admiral's uniform in *Skimmer*, she was still sleeping. When she awoke, well past eleven that night—Brenden had sent word that he would not, after all, be able to join them for dinner—she was astounded to learn that she'd slept the day away.

"I don't know why," she said. "I just don't know."

"Reaction, I guess," Pat said. "Now that the end is so near all the work and tension is catching up with you."

"Don't leave me, Pat. Not tonight."

He didn't. She fell asleep again, and he sat there beside her bed, dozing now and then, until well after dawn.

THIRTEEN

The Taratwo fleet, the most devastating instrument of destruction ever assembled, blinked as a unit to the area of operations. Aboard Corinne's flagship, Pat was in command. He had suggested to the Brenden that the first engagement should be according to existing naval strategy, based on the massed firepower of huge fleets. Later, he would try to come up with some variations to entertain the gunners of the Brenden's half of the fleet.

Everyone knew in advance the outcome of the first engagement. The previous exercises had proved beyond doubt that the disrupters could score at least one deadly hit on each enemy ship before conventional weapons began to take a toll.

Corinne seemed to be thinking of other things as Pat positioned his fleet in a traditional grid. From that formation the central-fire-control computer would direct the fire of small groups of ships on individual targets, the massed power of the lasers cutting through the shield of the targeted ship within less than two minutes. Ordinarily, it would have been a deadly strategy, for the fleet of over two thousand ships, firing in units of ten, would take out two hundred enemy ships in the first two minutes. The Brenden, seeing Pat's formation on the screens, arrayed his fleet in a long, thin bank which, as the range closed, began to adjust into a half crescent, so that the ships on the flanks could encircle Pat's formation and rake enfilading fire down the straight ranks of ships.

Pat walked forward to stand beside the gunner, Werner. Although Pat was dressed in the uniform of the Taratwo navy, Werner bowed his head quickly three times and looked at him adoringly.

"All is well?" Pat asked.

"Yes, Holiness," Werner said. Pat put his hand on the ugly yet graceful snout of the disrupter to feel its warmth. The secondary power was on. The weapon was alive, and the beam of power which came from the snout would not be that harmless stream of electrons which had been used previously in the exercises to allow the target ship's computer to register a hit.

"Your reward, Gunner Werner, will be great," he said, feeling his stomach turn at his own duplicity. Those beautiful young men were so eager, so easily influenced. When this was all over the mind scientists of the UP would spend years, decades, writing papers about the effects of repression of knowledge and specialized training in a closed society.

The small, controlled community on Dorchlunt was much like the weapon that the long-dead Zede scientists had developed. A series of impulses was injected into each, and those forces continued, around, and around, and around, until, in the case of the disrupter, the force was near the point of loss of control and came bursting out in the form of a burst of sheer energy of overwhelming power.

The human brain, being quite adaptable, could have, in the case of the closed system on Dorchlunt whose components were flesh and blood, continued to accept the forces enclosed for an unpredictable period. However, Pat felt, sooner or later that closed system, too, would have had to find release of its energies. Perhaps, given time, some young man like Gorben would have begun to question the thousand-year-old doctrine, or would have come up with some simple invention which would have been a minor but growing disruptive influence to the rule of the priests.

Now there would be no chance of that. Dorchlunt would not be the same after today.

The fleets closed, moving at a fraction of light speed on their flux drives. It would begin within minutes. Pat's stomach was acting up. He swallowed the desire to run for a sanitary cabinet to vomit up the fear and regret that had seemed to collect in his belly.

"Mr. Kelly," he said to the Taratwo fire control officer who would direct the fleet's conventional weapons, "you may fire when you are within range."

There were only three men, other than Pat and Corinne, on the bridge of the flagship. The trend in building ships of war had been, in the past decade, toward more computer control and smaller crews. The entire compliment of the flagship was just ten men.

Pat saw the flickering from afar, the small winking of the Brenden's lasers beginning, and heard his own conventional weapons open up at extreme range. The screens of his own ships were not even strained, and he knew the same was true for those of the Brenden.

He had to give no further orders to Werner, who, as flagship gunner, was coordinating the fire of the gunners throughout Pat's half of the fleet. He held his breath. Now the screens began to sizzle and indicators began to blink estimates of loss of screen power as the laser weapons began to take their toll—simulated, of course, for this was, after all, just a war game between elements of the same fleet.

Pat had to breathe. He looked doubtfully toward Werner's position. The disrupter installation could not be seen from the bridge. He checked the range. Why were the disrupters not firing? Damage was being done by the lasers.

A feeling of mixed relief and dulled acceptance came to him. The gunners were not going to obey the orders of the God Fleet Admiral Torga Bluntz, after all.

He looked at Corinne. Well, history would be his judge. Perhaps, in some distant day of sanity, they'd look back and write about the traiter Audrey Patricia Howe, who joined the forces of the dictator who threw the populated galaxy into a new Dark Age. And those future historians wouldn't even know that he'd tried, wouldn't know that at one particular moment in time, when it seemed that his desperate plan had failed, he felt relief and looked at a woman, the dictator's sister, with a hunger which, being projected into her own green eyes, set her face flushing and caused her to make a tentative movement toward him.

And then they fired.

With a clicking rush the counters began to tell of disrupter hits on the ships of the Brenden's fleet, and the flagship's computer began to go crazy with alarms and warnings even while indicating that the ranks of Pat's grid were being reduced with the same deadly efficiency that had been the mark of the disrupter gunners in previous exercises.

And in the midst of it, in the clicking rush of counters and the grim closing movement of the fleets, the Brenden's voice roaring, "Cease fire, Cease fire."

Corinne had leaped to her feet. Her face was white; one hand was at her throat. Kelly, the fire-control officer, and the other crew members at positions on the bridge had their own jobs and were not aware that the hits being registered were not made by harmless beams of electrons from the primary power source.

On both sides of the battle line men and ships were dying.

For a few seconds, before the fully armed disrupters began to fire, before the amazingly swift gunners began to play the game in earnest, Pat had thought that the closed system which was Dorchlunt had become too engorged with superstition and blind obedience. He had feared that the young men of Dorchlunt had decided to break out of the circle, to disobey the orders of the God Fleet Admiral Torga Bluntz, who, as they stood at ease on the parade ground on the previous day, had explained carefully that the time had come for them to return to glory, to go to Zede not weak in the flesh, but powerful in the spirit so as to accomplish the desired return of all to their past positions of power and glory.

The God Fleet Admiral Torga Bluntz had spoken in the way of the priests of Dorchlunt, using the centuries of tradition and discipline to order the cream of the young men of Dorchlunt to kill each other in the name of that perverted and polytheistic system of belief which had been originally instituted by Torga Bluntz.

But Pat Howe, impersonating the God Fleet Admiral Torga Bluntz, stood with his eyes full of tears as men died and hysterical voices screamed on the fleet's communication frequency and the odd ship or two zapped out of formation, and the glow of direct disrupter hits left the new and expensive toys of the dictator Brenden lifeless hulks in space, all electronics fused, all life gone.

And Pat Howe prayed. He hadn't prayed in awe and fear and pain in a long, long time, not since he had been a child, but now he prayed to the one God who had created it all, saying, "Let there be light." He prayed for forgiveness. He prayed that he had been right. He prayed that the lives of those young Dorchlunters had not been sacrificed in vain.

It began with the minute hand of the bridge chronometer at seven minutes past the hour. At nine minutes thirty seconds past the hour the two fleets fell silent. The initial exchange of disrupter fire had killed almost two thousand ships, and those few left alive continued to fire. The gunners had no way of knowing, short of seeing the glow of a hit, which ships were alive or dead, and so those who survived kept spraying the disrupters up and down lines and ranks and then began to pick off the few ships trying to break formation, and one by one the survivors died, until there were only two disrupters firing, and those two swept the blasted ships again and again until Pat picked up the communicator and said, "Gorben, Werner, enough."

Corinne had a look of horror on her face, a look which came nearer to not being beautiful than Pat could ever have imagined. The fire-control officer, Kelly, was half crouched over his console, looking first toward Pat, then toward the computer read-out on the screen.

The gunner, Werner, appeared on the bridge. And at that moment Kelly yelled something totally incomprehensible and reached for his side-arm. He did not have time to clear it from the holster before Werner's hand beam left a smoking hole in his uniform. The other crew members on the bridge, stunned, not knowing exactly what had happened, were dead before Pat could say, again, "Enough, Werner."

"I will see to the others, Holiness," Werner said.

"Don't kill them," Pat said. "Take their weapons and lock them up."

"Sir," Werner barked, and was gone.

Corinne's eyes were unbelievably wide. She looked at Pat. One hand was up, two fingers pressed against her upper lip. She screamed once, and a look of agony was there as she ran to the communicator.

"Brenden, Brenden," she cried, her voice strained. "Brendennnnn," she wailed, and fell limply into the chair.

"Admiral," said a young, tense voice on the communicator.

Pat stood across the console from Corinne. She didn't look up at him.

"Admiral Bluntz here, Gorben. You may report."

"I have taken the ship, Holiness."

"Very well," Pat said.

"Brenden," Corinne whispered.

"And the Brenden?" Pat asked.

"He is here, Holiness."

"Let him speak," Pat said. He handed the communicator to Corinne.

"Brenden?" she whispered.

"I'm here, Cory." The voice was not the ebullient one of old.

"Oh, Brenden," Corrinne sobbed.

"Yes, you can sure pick'em, little sister," Brenden said. "Pat, you there?"

"I'm here," Pat said.

"What now?" the Brenden asked.

"I want Gorben off your ship," Pat said.

"Then me, huh?" Brenden said, his meaning clear.

"Then you're free to go," Pat said.

"Go? Go where?"

"Back to Taratwo," Pat said.

"And what about you, little sister?" Brenden asked. "Were you with him?"

"No, no," Corinne sobbed.

"Does she go with me?" Brenden asked.

"That's up to her," Pat said. He looked at her. He felt a great sense of loss, for her eyes blazed with hate.

Her sobs ceased. "You—you—do you actually think . . ."

"I can only hope," Pat said. "But I guess love isn't that powerful, is it?"

Before she could answer, Werner was back, a smile on his face. "The crew is neutralized, Holiness," he said proudly, snapping into a salute. It was in that position that he died. He died with a laser beam cutting a hole directly into the bridge of his nose and into his brain. He died swiftly.

Corinne turned the weapon on Pat so quickly that he had no time to reach for his own. Indeed, he had no desire to reach for a weapon to be used against Corinne. He stood facing her, sadness welling up in him for Werner, and for all the thousands of Werner's counterparts who had died on the other ships, and for the loss of the woman whose emerald eyes blazed fire at him down the barrel of a handbeam.

"I'm sorry," Pat said. "I am truly sorry, honey."

Her head began to move back and forth, and a sound of agony came from her lips. He saw her fingers tighten, her hand go white on the weapon. And then she stopped trembling.

"I can't kill you," she whispered. "I can't."

"Thank you," Pat said.

"But why, Pat?" she asked. "Why?"

He shrugged. "I don't think you could understand if I told you, honey. Look. It's over. I wish you'd come with me, but I suspect you can't. Why don't you get into gear and we'll transfer you over to the other ship. The two of you can handle her to take her back to Taratwo."

"To wait for the forces of the UP to come and punish us?" she asked.

"I'm afraid they'll at least want to be sure there are no disrupters on the planet," Pat said.

A tear grew and rolled down her cheek. "We had it all, Pat," she whispered. "We had it all and you threw it away."

"Admiral," came Gorben's voice.

"Yes, Gorben," Pat said.

"I have, in compliance with your orders, totally destroyed the disrupter aboard this ship, and I am ready to join you, Holiness."

"Very well, Gorben," Pat said. "Carry on."

Corinne had holstered her weapon. He helped her get into space gear. She was grimly silent. And then, just before he lifted the helmet onto her head, she said, "Kiss me, Pat."

He kissed her lightly, and for a moment hope came to him. Maybe, someday—

Gorben and Corinne passed in space, and then Gorben was aboard Pat's ship and Pat had watched the hatch close on Brenden's ship. Gorben looked at Werner's body without emotion.

"I'm sorry about Werner," Pat said.

"He has gone to Zede, to his glory," Gorben said. "I envy him. I regret only, Holiness, that I am not with the others."

"In time," Pat said sadly, for it happened to all in time, and to some too soon. He sat down in the command chair. The thrusters on Brenden's ship were beginning to glow. Nothing to do now but go back and get the good old *Skimmer* and go home.

"Your orders, Admiral?" Gorben asked, standing tall.

"We'll go back to Dorchlunt in a few minutes, Gorben," Pat said. "I'm going to leave you in charge there until I come back, with others."

"And then to Zede?"

"Or better," Pat said, wondering what X&A and the eggheads would make of Dorchlunt, and what they'd do to integrate the remaining Dorchlunters into the UP. "It's all going to work out, Gorben. Trust me."

"Of course, Holiness," Gorben said.

Brenden's ship was moving. Pat felt a tightness in his throat. He would gladly have traded the galaxy and all its treasures for one small, curvy, auburn-haired girl.

Brenden's ship was moving across his bow, coming broadside.

"Holiness," Gorben said, "he is going to pass dangerously near."

"It's all right, Gorben," Pat said.

He couldn't take his eyes off the ship, for two reasons, the most painful being that she was on it. He held his finger poised over a certain button. He glanced over his shoulder. Gorben was gone. He reached for the communicator button to tell Gorben that everything was under control, but his finger never reached it, for at that moment all the weapons on Brenden's ship, obviously under central control, opened up. A swarm of missiles shot out, and the projectile weapons fired intelligent shells, and the deadly beams reached for Pat's ship, sizzling the shield even as he reversed the movement of his hand and his finger shot toward the button which would take the ship away from the missiles, projectiles, beams on a blink which he'd programmed into the navigation computer for just this eventuality.

The screen went with an electrical distortion which caused his hair to stand up, and then he was screaming as his finger hit the button and the ship slid into that nowhere which is a blink, for in that last instant before there was empty, clear space in front of his screens as he reemerged he had seen Brenden's ship glow.

He had screamed, "No, Gorben, no!"

Within minutes he was back, blinking his ship to within half a mile of the pride of the Taratwo fleet, the Brenden's flagship. The ship was as dead, as empty of any mechanical, electronic, or life-form impulse, as was the ancient colony ship which circled Dorchlunt. Gorben had been trained too well. In those few seconds he'd reached the disrupter, and in that split second between the firing of Brenden's weapons and the blink, his superb reaction time had allowed the beam of his disrupter to strike Brenden's flagship amidships.

FOURTEEN

The ways of the gods, Gorben thought, are very strange. They are not, however, to be questioned, even when a god does something as odd as inter two human bodies encased in boxes in the earth. He had the honor of being on the detail which helped the God Fleet Admiral Torga Bluntz remove the bodies of the red-headed ones from the dead ship, encase them in metal boxes fabricated in the shops from valuable, ancient material, and then bury them under six feet of the red earth of Dorchlunt.

Nor did Gorben question or doubt when the god used the weapons of his own little ship to destroy the last surviving Taratwo cruiser, with the last of the disrupters aboard.

"Admiral Bluntz," Gorben said, for, as the god had said, now everyone could speak the sacred name openly, much to the chagrin of the priesthood, "if I may be so bold, sir, will you return, in my own lifetime, or is your return, with those others of whom you speak, to be a matter of patience and generations as was the period of your first return?"

"In your lifetime, Gorben. A matter of weeks, at most. Greet those who come with friendship, Gorben. They will bring odd and wonderful things, and the life-style of the Dorchlunters will be altered forever."

"I await eagerly my ascent to glory," Gorben said.

The computer aboard the *Skimmer* was next to useless. Pat had to stay alert on the long trip home, as the ship blinked and blinked and then paused to charge. During the charge periods he slept with the aid of an intake of alcohol far beyond his customary habits. He did not drink the last two days before reaching Xanthos so that his head would be clear for his report. He asked specifically for Jeanny Thompson, needing, wanting, a friendly face as he told his incredible story.

A crusty X&A admiral, called in for the second telling of Pat's tale, grunted and said, "Has this man been given a psychological evaluation?" That was his way of saying he didn't believe. Pat didn't give a damn.

"Sir," he said, "I'll pass on the psychological evaluation. Just follow the blink route I've given Jeanny and you'll have your proof."

Almost five thousand ships dead in space was ample proof.

At last he was finished. He kept himself together long enough to lift the *Skimmer* to the shipyard and leave orders for that long-delayed overhaul. Then he tried his damnedest to disappear into a bottle.

When Jeanny Thompson finally found him she used her handbeam to cut the lock which he yelled out to her that he would not open.

"God, what a slob," she said, when she saw him.

She walked to the holo projector and stood behind it. A beautiful auburn-haired girl in period costume was frozen in time and space, standing at the head of a long, sweeping staircase.

"So that's Corinne," Jeanny said.

Then she took the cassette from the projector and opened a window and threw it out. It shattered into a thousand pieces on the pavement four stories below. Pat bellowed and charged at her drunkenly, and she clipped him neatly on the side of the neck and caught him before he fell.

When he awoke he was clean, his three-week-beard had been shaved, not too gently, and the apartment no longer reeked of stale sweat and booze. His head was clear.

"I used detox on you," Jeanny said.

"I don't thank you for it," Pat said. She had died within half a mile of him, that beautiful woman. She had died and—

"Hungry?" Jeanny asked.

"No," he said.

"Eat anyhow," Jeanny ordered, putting food in front of him. In spite of himself, the smell of it caused his stomach to growl.

"OK, Audrey," Jeanny said.

"Don't call me Audrey," he said, around a bite of delicious meat.

"You've spent a month feeling sorry for yourself. So you've lost your great love, the love of your life—"

The food turned to straw in his mouth. And his look caused Jeanny to hold up one hand quickly.

"Sorry," she said. "I won't do that again."

He chewed and swallowed.

"Pat, an X&A ship just got back from your planet. They found everything there just as you said it would be."

Pat nodded.

"There's a little difficulty with the natives, Pat. After all, they've had their beliefs for a thousand years. They're going to be in for a severe dose of culture shock."

"Can't be helped," Pat said.

"It can be eased," she said.

"I'm sure you people can handle it," Pat said.

"There's a young man named Gorben out there who says he won't obey any order against the old ways unless it comes directly from Fleet Admiral Torga Bluntz." She leaned forward. "Pat, I can't pretend that I know how you feel. Apparently I've never loved anyone like that, but I can imagine that you're still sore in your heart from having to let those beautiful blond young men kill each other."

"I am," Pat said.

"There are a few of them left," she said. "They need your help, Pat. Think of the things they're going to be hit with. They're going to learn that a thousand years of tradition have all been in vain, that Zede lost the war, that there's going to be no return to glory, no heaven in Zede."

"Any decent planet will seem like heaven after Dorchlunt," Pat said.

"Pat," she said accusingly.

"All right, dammit, what can I do? Haven't I done enough to them already?"

"You can go back, as Admiral Bluntz, and ease the blow a bit for them, help them make the transition."

"Alone?"

"No. X&A will have people swarming all over the place. That's a pretty mean weapon out there, Pat. They'll want to be sure that the secret doesn't get off Dorchlunt, and that there are no more working models in existence."

"I won't be a part of the service," Pat said. "I won't go out there on an X&A ship."

"I can sign a charter agreement for the *Skimmer*," she said. "It won't be at your usual exorbitant rates."

"I'll think it over," Pat said.

"Pat, the service can't force you to go. But you might find it a little rough to get clearances the next time you try to go into space. You might have a little trouble with your licenses."

"Blackmail," Pat said, but he was thinking of Gorben. The kid deserved better than he had coming.

"Call it what you will."

"OK. Draw me a charter. I'll go out on *Skimmer* and talk to them."

"Since this is an official mission, there'll have to be an X&A officer with you."

Pat shook his head, thinking of weeks in space with some brass-bound service egghead. "No deal. The deal is off. I will not have some hardass X&A joker on *Skimmer*."

"That's odd," Jeanny said. "I thought my ass was pretty soft."

"You?" he asked.

"That's my assignment."

Well, that wouldn't be bad. Jeanny was a decent sort. He'd rather be alone, but if it had to be anyone, better Jeanny than anyone else.

He put her in the mate's cabin. The *Skimmer* gleamed. The old man, the computer, was as sharp as new. Jeanny didn't push herself on him. She alternated watches with him, although it wasn't really necessary, and she spoke only when spoken to. He found himself comparing her with Corinne. Corinne was more beautiful, but Jeanny wasn't bad, not bad at all, and she was an old friend and she'd gone on the line for him a couple of times. No reason to take it out on her.

One night as they waited for the generator to charge he found himself talking to her about Corinne. She made little sympathetic sounds.

She cleaned up the mate's cabin. It wasn't all that bad having her aboard. She was neat, and she didn't talk all the time. One day, halfway to Dorchlunt, she made him laugh.

They blinked out near the planet Dorchlunt in what was, for Pat, an unfortunate position. Brenden's flagship, dead in space, had been left in an orbit just slightly higher than that of the old colony ship, and as it happened both ships were in sight when *Skimmer* emerged. Pat felt a twist of his heart. It was night in the villages. Pat suggested they get a good sleep before going down at dawn. He dreamed of that last moment when he realized that Gorben had made his way to the disrupter and, thinking that he was defending his god, had turned the disrupter on the ship which contained Brenden and Corinne. He awoke, and there was a soft hand on his forehead, and a soft voice saying, "Hey, take it easy, old buddy."

"Corinne?"

"No, just me," Jeanny said.

"Ah, God," he said, his voice choking, and when she clasped her arms around his head and pulled his cheek down to her bare, hot breasts, he did not protest, but let the nightmare continue, and then there were tears in his eyes and then worse. He wept.

When he had expended himself Jeanny still held him. "My boy," she said, "I don't know whether to be glad or sorry that you never loved me that much. It would be flattering, in a way, and a huge burden in another, you know?"

He pulled away, kissed her on the cheek. "Thanks, Jeanny," he said.

"Want company the rest of the night?" she asked.

He didn't say anything. She crawled into the bed beside him, put her arms around him. He didn't move, but he didn't try to push her away. She was warm and soft against him, but he felt no desire for her. His desire had died with that sleek ship which orbited the planet above the old relic. Jeanny, concerned for him, said, "Hey, if there's anything at all that I can do—"

He was touched, but he said, "I'm dead inside."

"Want me to go back to my own bunk?" she asked. "I'm not especially trying to seduce you, Audrey, I just thought that, well, a little companionship, a little something. Maybe just a holding, a hugging, a touching. It's a damned big galaxy out there, Audrey, and it dwarfs hell out of us sometimes, doesn't it? Sometimes I think we need to have someone close, someone just to touch, or hold on to. What do you think?"

"I don't know," Pat said in a dead voice.

She took her arms from around him, sat on the side of the bed. "Audrey," she whispered.

"Don't—" He didn't finish. That was three times she'd called him Audrey and he couldn't even make a comeback. He was, she knew, hurting like hell.

"Audrey," she said, "I'd like to know just one thing. I know those new Zede-built cruisers. One man, unless he's very, very fast and has four arms, would have a difficult time flying a ship and manning the arms-control console at the same time. Am I right?"

The sound he made was not a word.

She couldn't decide, for a moment, whether it was best to pursue that line of thinking or to leave him to his pain. She decided on the radical incision, the thrust to his heart.

"Pat, who was sitting at arms control when you boarded the ship?" She held her breath, fearing a violent reaction from him. He answered her question in an indirect way. His hand closed over her wrist and pulled, and his grip was strong, almost painful. She let him pull her down beside him, and as his arms closed around her, as she adjusted her warmth to his body, she knew.

"I'm going to say it, Pat," she whispered. "I know it hurts, but it has to be said. It was Corinne who was on fire control, wasn't it? Pat, her last living act was to try to kill you."

He felt all twisted inside, felt as if something quite physical and terribly wrong was eating him. He clung to the soft warmth of another human being, felt her breath in his face.

She knew that he was not deliberately trying to hurt her, but he held her so tightly that she had difficulty breathing. Then, after a long, long time, he relaxed his grip on her a bit, and she snuggled into a more comfortable position. "All right?" she asked him.

"Thanks, friend," he said.

He held her until she went to sleep, her breath soft in his face, and he held her as if the woman's warmth of her was all that kept him from sliding down into a blackness deeper and more lonely than the space around him.

EPILOGUE

As Jeanny had promised, X&A technicians and social scientists swarmed over the lonely Dorchlunt. A ship's tailor shop had outfitted Pat with several copies of the ancient Zede uniform which he'd taken from the statue of Admiral Bluntz, and Pat was a busy man for weeks. Gorben was at his side constantly, and the young man surprised Pat by adapting to the totally different circumstances in which he found himself with a stoic acceptance.

A few of the older Dorchlunters, faced with cultural shock which negated all their beliefs, chose suicide, clinging to one last hope of going to Zede. Pat sat in on the conference where it was determined that it would be best for the Dorchlunt survivors to be settled on a thinly populated agricultural planet at several parsecs distance. Pat, in his pose as the admiral, had the not too pleasant job of telling Gorben and the others that they would be moved away from the only planet they'd ever known.

He was in his quarters alone that night when Gorben knocked politely and came in to stand at attention until Pat ordered him to sit.

"Sir," Gorben said, "we are sad."

"It's going to be fine," Pat said. "You'll be living on a fine world. There'll be rich soil. You will have an island to yourselves. You will be taught by the people of X&A to live in modern society."

"If you are there, perhaps we can cope," Gorben said.

Pat cleared his throat. He'd been on Dorchlunt too long. He was constantly reminded of Corinne. The dead fleet still lay in near space, the bodies still aboard, for it would require a major effort to provide burials, and it was more important at the moment to help the living. He felt guilty because he had not planned to accompany the Dorchlunters to the new planet, and he was the one who had given the orders which resulted in the death of most of Dorchlunt's young men.

It was going to be a very difficult transition. X&A would provide tools and the basic living necessities, but the work ethic was still very much alive in UP society. There'd be no free ride for the Dorchlunters. There was nothing he could do.

Or was there?

He picked up the communicator. Jeanny was in conference with other X&A brass. "Jeanny," he said, "I need a little time to myself. I'm going to take *Skimmer* and take a look around the area. I'll be back in a few days." He closed the communicator before Jeanny could protest. "Come alone, son," he told Gorben; "let's take a little ride."

He found the Brenden's flagship quickly. The coordinates of that last battle were burned into his brain. He told Gorben to stay on the *Skimmer*, suited up, made the transfer to the dead ship.

Murphy's Stone sat in airless solitude in the

case which had been made for it, powerless laser snout almost touching it. In Pat's light it sparkled in extravagant splendor.

It took three days to make the right contacts once *Skimmer* had landed on Zede. He escorted Gorben for the boy's first glimpse of what was supposed to be heaven, and Gorben was more than ready to leave once the transaction had been concluded.

"Will there be as many people in our new home?" Gorben asked, when *Skimmer* was back in space.

"No. You'll have privacy."

And they'd have many other things. They'd have a corps of agricultural experts to teach them. They'd have the most advanced farming equipment, good homes, and as they learned the ways of modern society they'd have any of the luxuries that they wanted.

The old man who had found the huge diamond was dead, the first victim of the Brendens' ambition. The Brendens were dead. A peacekeeping force was occupying Taratwo. No one owned Murphy's Stone, and Pat, although he'd dreamed a few dreams of what he could do with the money it had brought on Zede, didn't know of a better use for the money than to assure a future for Gorben and the others.

There would be times, later, after he and Jeanny had made a leisurely and enjoyable trip home and he'd almost immediately accepted a new commission, that he'd kick himself. And there would be times when he felt that he'd tried to buy off his conscience by setting up the trust for the Dorchlunters with the proceeds of the sale of Murphy's Stone; but the old man was as crisp and sharp as a young computer, the *Skimmer* had enjoyed a total overhaul, and there were new films in the library. He knew that there was a price to pay for everything, and he felt good about himself.